PRAISE FOR ROBERT

GOOD PEOPLE

"Lopez's methodical narrators will draw comparisons to Beckett, but they also share DNA with the Austrian writer Thomas Bernhard, showcasing out-of-touch anxiety cases in all their poetically elliptical glory.... Lopez has the ability to give the reader whiplash with his unconventional and bewitching stories."

—*Los Angeles Times*

"Read [*Good People*] to stumble into the sunlight afterward.... Depressing, inventive, and marvelous—a thought-provoking path to feeling awful."

—*Kirkus Reviews* (starred review)

"Tightly knit.... Recommended for lovers of darkly humorous, strangely illuminating fiction."

—*Booklist*

"Personalities ranging from the amusingly neurotic to the borderline psychotic shape the twenty quirky stories in this collection.... Lopez shows uncommon skill at evoking both laughs and shudders, sometimes in the same story."

—*Publishers Weekly*

"Lopez uses a close point of view to maximum effect, drawing the reader into each character's mindset; despite the sense of complicity this imparts, the dark humor and discomfort of these stories provides just as much enlightenment."

—*Late Night Library*

"A dizzying, disturbing tour of what might be going on in the minds of 'good people'.... Those who enjoy dark humor with a dose of sado-masochistic sexual fantasy will take pleasure in [Lopez's] spare prose and ability to spear a thought on first strike."

—*Foreword Reviews*

"Robert Lopez's strange, incantatory, visionary stories reveal the mysteries behind the ordinary world. You lift your head from this book and it's as if a third eye has been opened."

—Dan Chaon, author of *Await Your Reply* and *Stay Awake*

"Robert Lopez is such a master of saddening hilarities that his virtuoso turns in this crazily heartbreaking, dizzyingly original new collection will restore even the most jaded reader's faith in the fresh possibilities of American fiction."

—Gary Lutz, author of *Stories in the Worst Way*

"Robert Lopez is the master of deadpan dread, of the elliptical koan, of the sudden turn of language that reveals life to be so wonderfully absurd. Always with Lopez, the voice is all his—enchanting, surprising, at times devastating."

—Jess Walter, author of *Beautiful Ruins*

"[Lopez's] prose flows with such natural ease and liquid pronunciation that he makes the difficult seem very easy. Mixing in the wordplay of Samuel Beckett and the flat humor of writers like Stephen Dixon and Salinger, his work is a delight and a provocation."

—Blake Butler, author of *300,000,000* and *There Is No Year*

"[Lopez's world] is an affectless poetics planet caught in the black-hole gravity of a Stephen Dixon-esque free-falling narrative sink."

—Michael Martone, author of *Four for a Quarter* and *The Blue Guide to Indiana*

ASUNDER

"If Lopez's earlier books didn't prove to readers that he is a word-storm, a force of literary nature come unhinged, blowing shutters against readers' houses, then *Asunder* surely will. This is a collection as proof, a collection as loveliness, a collection as rippage, and we are lucky to get it into our waiting hands, its words into our heads."

— *The Rumpus*

"[Lopez] indulges in monologues, daydreams, and narrative meanderings, the sentences firing off and ending like flash messages between synapses...that's why it was such a thrill and a pleasure to read."

— *The Literary Review*

"Lopez confronts the world of page-long descriptions and destroys the notion that a good story needs to be overly saturated.... The opposite could be said of the stories in *Asunder*. In a world of noise, Lopez offers quiet. There is a tremendous restraint to the language in the collection. The prose is simple and powerful; it reminds the reader that sometimes more is conveyed in silences."

—*Ampersand Books*

"Admirers of the short-short form will appreciate this collection. With perfection in phrasing and attention to the minutiae of prose, Asunder presents a model for how new the English language can seem. There is nothing tried or tired here." —*NewPages*

KAMBY BOLONGO MEAN RIVER

"Brutally funny and bleak, yet invested with an intense, sweet sadness, *Kamby Bolongo Mean River* crackles with the energy of a writer performing brilliantly. In a small miracle, the pleasures of that performance never obstruct the narrative. Lopez's story about broken language is finally most powerful for a character we cannot confidently name, who has lived a life we cannot outline, in places we do not understand."

—*Review of Contemporary Fiction*

"*Kamby Bolongo Mean River* is an original and fearless fiction. It bears genetic traces of Beckett and Stein, but Robert Lopez's powerful cadences and bleak, joyful wit are all his own."

—Sam Lipsyte, author of *Homeland* and *The Ask*

"Reading *Kamby Bolongo Mean River* is like reading *The Catcher in the Rye* for the first time; you just know something momentous is happening as you read, as you become drawn in to Lopez's bizarre, fractured narrative."

—*New York Journal of Books*

"*Kamby Bolongo Mean River* is fluid and funny and moving on a first read, but its exploration of existence and isolation gets smarter, funnier, and deeper every time I read it.... First, the prose is as clear as can be, with a lot of air in it, a lightness, and the rhythm and variation in the repetition make for a kind of beautiful song. The other reason *Kamby*'s not oppressive is because it's so funny on the page, maybe the funniest book I've ever read."

—*The Lit Pub*

"The tenderness with which Lopez treats these fragile characters, the honesty in their rendering, the lullaby of loneliness that coos through this world, whispering along the banks of the Kamby Bolongo and above the rooftops of Injury, Alaska; Johnny's longing, his fear, his isolation—all of these are pure Lopez."

—*The Brooklyn Rail*

"In his second novel, Robert Lopez once again taps a deeply comedic voice.... A narrative within the narrative takes shape, a prelinguistic one reminiscent of prehistoric cave paintings. He is tracing back toward the origin of his voice. He has a plan, and as the brilliant pacing and rhythm of the narrative drive toward its conclusion, this excellent novel forces a reconsideration of the very concept of a native language."

—*The Quarterly Conversation*

"In examining confinement the novel certainly telegraphs the stark spirit of Samuel Beckett's later writings, yet Lopez's innovative meditation on isolation is singular in its grim humor and emotional influence. Framed by the obsessively bizarre yet sincere outlook of a young man held under observation in unknown environs, *Kamby Bolongo* is a mesmeric interpretation of words: 'what is between the words and behind them.'" —*Bookslut*

"Form reflects subject here: this is a story at full steam, one that cannot be bogged down by traditional conventions.... *Kamby Bolongo Mean River* begs to be read in one sitting, and the syntax—the hypnotic looping, the relentless unpacking of sentences—reverberates long after the novel is put down."

—*360 Main Street*

"Robert Lopez's carefully crafted, insistent prose is matched by his bold exploration of madness, abuse, emotional and psychological trauma, isolation, but also of one man's self-motivated, if still ill-directed, plan for rehabilitation. *Kamby Bolongo Mean River* may just tie both your brain and stomach into knots."

—*Word Riot*

"*Kamby Bolongo Mean River* constantly haunts my desk, no matter how many times I try to return it to the shelves.... A character in possession of one of the most uniquely rendered and affecting modes of speech in recent memory. By the end of the novel, the narrator is still in the same place he was in the same place as the beginning, but I'm willing to bet that no reader—no listener, for this novel is as much spoken as it is written—will be able to say the same."

—*Post Road*

"Through astonishingly organic and layered language, Robert Lopez has created an inner world so remarkable you might fall over with fright, and then stay on the floor to laugh a while."

—*Southeast Review*

PART OF THE WORLD

"Robert Lopez has written a darkly hilarious exploration of the trickery of memory, the unreliability of personal history, and the strangeness, even uncanniness, of our daily transactions. As we follow Lopez's hapless narrator about the business of trying to navigate his homely part of the world, we are made to reconsider our own well-mapped relations, the unhygienic corners of our homes."

—Dawn Raffel, author of *The Secret Life of Objects*

"Reading *Part of the World* by Robert Lopez felt to me like standing in front of one of those marvelous, mind-bending exhibits at the Museum of Jurassic Technology that seem at first glance to be doing exactly nothing and at second glance to be dissolving and reconstituting reality as we thought we knew it. Literary pleasures like this are all too uncommon."

—Laird Hunt, author of *Neverhome* and *Kind One*

"In his first novel, Robert Lopez leads the reader into a peculiar part of the world on his own terms. The novel itself deals with the everyday actions.... However, these tasks become yard sticks by which one must measure the narrator himself and his sense of reality."

—*Verse*

ALL BACK FULL

ALL BACK FULL

A NOVEL IN THREE ACTS

ROBERT LOPEZ

DZANC BOOKS

5220 Dexter Ann Arbor Rd.
Ann Arbor, MI 48103
www.dzancbooks.org

Library of Congress Cataloging-in-Publication Data

Names: Lopez, Robert, 1971- author.
Title: All back full : a novel in three acts / Robert Lopez.
Description: First edition. | Ann Arbor, MI : Dzanc Books, 2017.
Identifiers: LCCN 2016017549 | ISBN 9781941088678
Subjects: LCSH: Nonverbal communication--Fiction. | Interpersonal
    relations--Fiction. | Oral communication--Fiction.
Classification: LCC PS3612.O65 A79 2017 | DDC 813/.6--dc23
LC record available at https://lccn.loc.gov/2016017549

First US edition: February 2017
Book design by Michelle Dotter

Printed in the United States of America

10   9   8   7   6   5   4   3   2   1

ALL BACK FULL

ACT I

The setting is an ordinary setting. A kitchen. One table and four chairs. A counter with a sink. Cabinets across the room from the table and chairs. A door that opens into the kitchen.

The principals are at the table. They are married to each other.

The man is middle-aged. He can be tall or short, but is probably not thin. He is portly, but not rotund. He can be bald or have a full head of hair. If he has hair, some of it is gray, but not all of it. He is not the sort for all of his hair to be gray. It is certainly not silver.

He can be any ethnicity. Say, for now, he is a white man. Another time he might be black or brown or some other color.

The woman is anywhere from thirty to fifty years of age. She is taller than her husband and probably younger, but not much younger. They are contemporaries, sharing similar histories and backgrounds. She can rest her chin on the top of his head. Years ago they'd perform this trick at parties. They called it a trick even though it is not a trick.

Past that she is not at all distinctive.

The man is reading a newspaper. This is a time when people still read newspapers. It might be Sunday. In fact, it probably is Sunday. It is Sunday morning.

The woman is also reading a newspaper. It is the same newspaper. They are trading sections back and forth. She enjoys the magazine, the week in review.

They do not read a daily newspaper. They do not sit down at the table to read the newspaper together every morning, trading sections back and forth. The subscription is for the Sunday edition, though sometimes it takes them all week to read it.

He will sometimes bring a section to the park with him. He will sit on a bench and try to read. Most often he is unable to concentrate.

The other people distract him, as he is easily distractible.

She tries to find time at work to read certain stories she couldn't finish on Sunday. She does this during lunch or on breaks but never during actual work-time.

The table has on it two coffee mugs and a plate of breakfast pastries. We can presume that one or the other woke early this morning and drove to the bakery.

It is not important which principal drove to the bakery.

For the sake of fair play, let's presume they take turns doing this, alternating Sundays. Let's say that today it was the husband's turn to drive to the bakery.

They read like this for a time.

It is quiet. There is no sound, save the occasional sip of coffee, the placing of a mug back down on the table or the turning of a page.

This quiet goes on for what might seem like a long time. It might feel like five minutes or months or years.

How the time feels depends upon if you are the man or the woman or someone observing the man and woman.

Finally, the man says, without looking up, Was that your friend? The woman says, It was, also without looking up. The man says, How is she? The woman says, The same.

It is quiet again. They look up and at each other, maybe past each other or through.

The man says, The same as always? The woman says, The same as ever.

They go back to reading.

The man is asking after the woman's friend. He is curious about this friend as she is something of a new friend for the woman. The woman has any number of friends but this is a new one. He has only met this friend once or twice and isn't sure how he feels about her.

The man doesn't have any new friends. He'll make new acquaintances as people do in the course of living a daily life, mixing with people at work and in public, but these never turn into friends. No one he can make plans with, no one he can call on for counsel or aid.

He has only the one friend, the same one he's had for years.

This friend is coming over later.

This will likely be a problem for everyone, particularly the woman.

But neither principal is thinking about this now. Now the man is thinking about the woman's new friend and the woman is thinking about something else.

The man heard the telephone ring earlier and assumed it was the woman's new friend. They seem to talk on the telephone once or twice a month, always on Sunday mornings.

The man thinks this is intrusive and presumptuous.

No one else calls on Sundays, let alone in the morning.

The man says, Was she naked?
The woman says, When?
The man says, When you spoke with her?
The woman says, I think she was. Yes.
The man says, Did you ask if she was naked?
The woman says, No, I forgot to.
The man says, Did you forget or did it not occur to you?
The woman says, What's the difference?

This is a short pause because the man likes to think about certain questions, pondering the whys and wherefores. He enjoys nuance and language and the language of nuance.

He likes to think about time and how it can feel like five minutes or days or years, depending upon everything and nothing all at once.

The man says, I'm not sure.
The woman says, Neither am I.

They go back to reading. It seems as if this conversation is over.

When it says *they go back to reading*, this isn't entirely true. The woman does indeed go back to reading. She is in the middle of a feature about the proprietor of a new business downtown that combines industrial design and Zen meditation.

The woman is invested in her local community and feels like a part of it. She is a part of it. She is known around town as someone who is part of the community. She has always wanted to know what was going on, who was doing what and where they were doing it and who it was inconveniencing. She volunteers. She contributes.

The man, however, is not actually reading. The newspaper is open in front of him, but he is not reading it.

The man says, I suppose one implies something and the other doesn't.

The woman says, What does?

The man says, Forgetting and failing to realize. Oblivion, or rather, obliviousness. Obsolescence, if you will.

The woman says, I won't, thank you.

The man says, One implies forethought, intention, or something to that effect. To forget something is to have once remembered it. To have once concentrated, considered…at least, you take note of it. You walk down the street and look at a tree. Maybe you don't study the tree or examine the tree, you don't consider the make or model or how old the tree is, but you notice the tree. You look at the tree and you register a tree. The rest of the world falls away in that moment. Failing to realize something is ignorance or a kind of ignorance. It's walking past the tree and not even seeing it. It's not being aware of what is going on around you. This is what I mean by oblivion. I think this is right.

The woman says, Genus.

The man says, I wouldn't call it genius, per se, but it's close.

The woman says, There is nothing close to genius. Genius is absolute, like…pregnancy. It's like death. The rest of the world falls away when you die, not when you look at a tree. I have never been so enthralled with a tree that I…

She loses her place in the conversation and then regains it. This takes maybe four or five seconds.

The man has learned to be patient whenever these displacements occur. Years ago he would try reminding her of what it is they were discussing, where he thought she was going, what she was about to say or trying to say. He learned to stop doing this after she cursed at him during a dinner party. She said, Don't ever fucking tell me what I'm about to say, you presumptuous fuck.

Maybe she didn't actually say this at the dinner party, but this is how he remembers it.

What she probably said at the dinner party was, Excuse me?

It was how she said it and where it was said and who got to hear it and what they might think.

The woman continues, I don't think anyone else has, either. Maybe dendrophiles, if there is such a thing. I'm sure there is. I read yesterday that a man was caught having sex with his car. It was in the newspaper. Not *in* his car, but *with* his car. Do you understand what I'm telling you? He was having relations with an automobile. Apparently it had been going on for years, this affair with a car. Of course, they didn't disclose the gentleman's name. Or the car's, for that matter. I can't remember what kind…it's all the same. This is the world we live in now. Men fuck cars and they report this in the newspaper. We deem it newsworthy.

While the woman did read this in the newspaper, it is probably important to note that it wasn't yesterday's newspaper, but rather last Sunday's edition.

However, it is possible she read this in a magazine at the doctor's office. Yesterday the woman went to the doctor. She experiences pain in her head and jaw, one whole side of it. She's felt this pain for years. She doesn't know what's wrong with her and neither do the doctors.

Otherwise, she overheard someone saying this about the man and his car while at the doctor's office or any of the myriad public places she's been this past week.

It's also possible she saw this on television. There might have been some kind of human freak show on one of the so-called learning or discovery channels having to do with aberrant behavior and sexuality.

Paraphilia describes the experience of intense sexual arousal to highly atypical objects, situations, or individuals. Examples include sexual interests that can motivate one into committing sexual offences—such as pedophilia, zoophilia, sexual sadism, and exhibitionism—but also include many harmless sexual interests, such as transvestism. There is no consensus for any precise border between unusual personal sexual tastes and paraphilic ones, and multiple, overlapping definitions exist. There is debate over which, if any, of the paraphilias should be listed in diagnostic manuals, such as the Diagnostic and Statistical Manual of Mental Disorders (DSM) or the International Classification of Diseases.

It is not known how many different kinds of paraphilias exist; one source lists as many as 549 paraphilias.

Both trees and automobiles are on this list.

The man says, It is our collective concern.

This comment, that it is our collective concern, is not altogether true. The man sometimes feigns concern. The man sometimes pretends to care about certain issues of the day, what goes on in the neighborhood, injustices both here and abroad, but the truth is he doesn't care. He knows he is supposed to care, but he doesn't. He has never written a letter, signed a petition, or protested anything. He has never marched. He has never been arrested.

He has never done anything on anyone's behalf.

Sometimes the woman invites him along on one of her community endeavors. She tells him that it's good to help others. She mentions altruism and karma.

The man says, I'd like to help.

The woman looks at him. He looks back. They continue looking at each other like this for five minutes or days or years. Then she walks away. He calls out to her, says, Have fun or Be careful or Everyone appreciates this.

The man would like for everything in the world to be just and fair, for everyone to be equal.

He thinks most of the efforts to accomplish these things are futile. He thinks the people who lead the charge are fools, as are the people who follow.

He calls them bangers.

He says this to his one friend, the one who is coming over later. He says, The bangers were out in full force today.

He says, One could hear the drums from across the stree across the city proper, from across the universe divide.

His one friend agrees with him whenever he goes on like this. Later he is coming over to drink and maybe watch the baseball game. It's possible he will stay for dinner.

This friend chews on toothpicks, carries them around in a case.

This friend used to smoke cigarettes, but quit years ago.

The man can't remember if the friend chewed on toothpicks at the same time he was smoking cigarettes. As such, he's not sure if the toothpicks serve as some kind of oral substitute.

The man told the woman that his friend might come over to drink and maybe watch the baseball game. He said it was possible he might stay for dinner.

He wasn't sure if this was a good idea.

He wasn't sure if having the friend over was a good idea and he wasn't sure that telling his wife the friend was coming over was a good idea, either.

He said this yesterday while she was on her way to march for pedestrian safety.

Last week two children, a brother and sister, were run over and killed by a reckless driver. The children were walking on the sidewalk when a truck jumped the curb and pinned them against the side of a building. This happened in front of their mother, who was busy tying the shoelace of another child. To the woman this is unimaginable, every part of it.

The woman cannot imagine conceiving, carrying to term, bearing and then rearing a child, let alone more than one, then watching this child or these children get killed by a truck in the middle of the day.

The march lasted two hours and probably did no good at all.

She told him she didn't think it was a good idea, the friend coming over for dinner.

She told him next time he should think.

Sometimes the man doesn't think. The man knows this about himself and considers it a problem.

Sometimes the man and woman agree with each other.

The man doesn't think of his wife as a banger. He likes that she is a good woman, that she has a big heart.

He doesn't think the woman knows all of this about him, but she does. The woman knows almost everything about him.

The man has never tried transvestism, which is something she probably knows.

He is sure that trying on one of his mother's skirts when he was a teenager doesn't qualify.

He's never applied makeup in his life, nor has he worn women's jewelry or shoes or even tried these on for size. Nor has he ever been tempted to do so.

He wanted to see how he looked and what it felt like to wear a skirt, which is the beginning and end of it.

He wishes his was a culture that allowed men to wear kilts or tunics.

The woman says, Surely someone is giving it to a tree right now. Somewhere in a thick forest with no one around to help, a dendrophile is putting the wood to an unsuspecting sycamore. He is fondling leaves, caressing bark, whispering sweet nothings. Maybe this has been going on for years. Maybe this is common knowledge. All of this car and tree-fucking.

The man says, We'd have heard something.

The woman says, I don't know if that's true.

The man says, We'd have seen something in the papers.

The woman says, This sort of thing has always gone unreported.

The woman is right about this, about this sort of thing going unreported in the past. But it's no longer the case. Now everything is reported. There are no secrets anymore, no filters.

Both of them know this, but don't want to discuss it because it saddens them.

The woman says, Poplars, redwoods, compacts, sedans, a shade tree, a fall-down tree. Someone somewhere is mounting a fall-down tree as we speak. An innocent little fall-down tree, minding its own fall-down business, is being violated right this very minute. And it doesn't bother me at all. Not in the slightest. This is what I'm telling you. I accept this. And I said genus before, not genius. Genus of trees, like...

The man says, I heard you the first time. It's all the same.

The woman says, It is all the same.

It seems as if they agree on this, that it is all the same, that everything is the same, but it's not clear if they do actually agree with each other about the sameness of everything. Sometimes it's easier if they agree with each other during a particular conversation and save up their disagreements for a better time.

Everything is the same, yes, and at the same time different. It is the same with time. They both know this.

The principals met at a mutual friend's going away party.

It is probably important to note this, to trace their history. People like to know how things begin, how they got started. People want to know the whole story.

Perhaps it is unnecessary, the whole story, as it won't explain everything, won't be at all satisfactory, in the end. But not everything needs explanation, not everything need be satisfactory.

If it is not important to trace their history in the grand scheme and big picture, then it is something to do. It is a way to pass the time.

This is what life comes down to, if it comes down to anything.

People have to pass the time the same way they pass the breakfast pastry, the Op-Ed section.

In today's Op-Ed section there's a piece that says there is no grand scheme, no big picture.

Today this qualifies as news.

The friend was going away soon, the next day, in the morning. It doesn't matter where the friend was going. The friend was going away from the man and woman and the place where they all lived. She had planned on returning, though, on picking up her life where she was hoping to leave it, maybe in a year or so. It's not clear how this affected the feeling of her going away. She was, indeed, going somewhere else, someplace definitive, someplace overseas. The man thought about this, thought about the notion of going away. Other people go away, people in relation to you, but you yourself never go away, you go somewhere else. The man may've said this at the going away party. He may've said this while everyone was drinking and enjoying themselves. The man was likewise drinking and enjoying himself but this is how he does such things. Not everyone responds to his philosophical inquiries, as they often seem rhetorical. Only once in a while will someone contribute to conversations he starts like this. On this night, however, the woman agreed with him and they talked for a couple of hours, discussing matters both great and small.

After this going away party, the man and woman retreated to separate corners. A week went by where nothing in the world happened. Then the woman went to the doctor for a minor procedure. She was to have something removed. It was nothing to worry about. The whole thing would take an hour, maybe two. Better to take care of it now. She'd get released the same day. It was outpatient, local anesthesia, didn't even need anyone to drive her there or back. She was ambulatory.

Then there were complications, but nothing too complicated. She had to have another procedure. Again nothing to worry about. This time they got it all. This time she had her sister drive her both there and back. She stayed that night with the sister. They tried to watch a movie together, but the woman fell asleep. It was the medication.

Before long, she was back to her normal routine.

This is when the man called and they made plans.

The man says, What the hell is a fall-down tree?

The woman says, I have no idea.

The man says, You made it up.

The woman says, I think I heard it in a song once. She sings, *You gotta meet me by the fall-down tree.* I think that's right. It might be a tree that has fallen down.

The man says, Do trees fall down?

The woman says, That's a good question. I should think anything alive and upright can fall down.

The man says, I would think most trees are felled.

The woman says, By tree-fuckers.

They go back to reading. They take sips of coffee. The man takes a bite out of a breakfast pastry, the flakes of which crumble all over the plate and onto the table. The man uses his right hand to sweep the flakes over to the side of the table and then off of it and into his left hand. He brushes his hands together so that the flakes fall directly onto the plate.

He says, I'd bet Joyce Kilmer was a tree-fucker. I bet he had a tree in every port. She says, Joyce Kilmer was definitely a tree-fucker, a tree-fucking dendrophile.

He says, How does one...(he then makes a fist and mimes a punching motion)...a car?

She says, I don't want to think about it.

He says, Would it be the tailpipe?

She says, Please.

He says, The car couldn't be running.

She says, I said please.

He says, This is something that's never occurred to me.

This is true. The man has never considered having sex with an automobile. He has imagined having sex with many people, including friends and coworkers, strangers and acquaintances, aunts and cousins, cripples and dwarfs. He has imagined sex with a transsexual, a woman who was once a man, but never the other way around. He thinks he might enjoy sex with a woman who was once a man. He is curious. He has never been curious about having sex with a man who was once a woman, nor has he ever imagined having sex with a man at all, though it might depend upon what one considers sex. The man has imagined performing certain acts or having certain acts performed on him, but that is the entirety of what he has imagined. He has heard about men having sex with animals but he has never imagined having sex with an animal. He doesn't think he'd be able to perform sex with an animal. Yet he doesn't pass judgment on those who have. He cannot imagine what it might be like to have a sheep, for instance, tempt one into sexual expression. He cannot imagine how long without human company one would have to go for a sheep to arouse this sort of interest. Still, if he had to have sex with an animal, if someone put a gun to his head, he thinks he'd choose a dolphin. They seem clean and of good temperament.

The plans included dinner and perhaps a drink after dinner. The man knew of a good place for a nightcap. It was quiet and out of the way. They could talk. It would be romantic.

Almost all dolphins are aggressive toward each other, and the older a male dolphin is, the more likely his body is covered with bite scars. Male dolphins engage in these aggressive acts apparently for the same reasons as humans: disputes between companions and competition for females. Acts of aggression can become so intense that targeted dolphins sometimes go into exile after losing a fight.

Male bottlenose dolphins have been known to engage in infanticide. Dolphins have also been known to kill porpoises for reasons that are not fully understood, as porpoises generally do not share the same diet as dolphins and are therefore not competitors for food.

Dolphin copulation happens belly to belly; though many species engage in lengthy foreplay, the actual act is usually brief, but may be repeated several times within a short span. They usually become sexually active at a young age, even before reaching sexual maturity. The age of sexual maturity varies by species and gender. Dolphins are known to display non-reproductive sexual behavior, engaging in masturbation, stimulation of the genital area of other individuals using the rostrum or flippers, and homosexual contact. Various species of dolphin have been known to engage in sexual behavior up to and including copulation with dolphins of other species. Sexual encounters may be violent, with male dolphins sometimes showing aggressive behavior toward both females and other males. Male dolphins may also work together and attempt to herd females in estrus, keeping the females close by means of both physical aggression and intimidation, to increase their chances of reproductive success.

Dolphins go back about ten million years, according to the fossil record. Occasionally, dolphins behave sexually toward other animals, including humans.

The man doesn't know all of this about dolphins, but he suspects most of it.

That week had the woman at the gym every morning, running on a treadmill. She was eager to regain her strength after the two procedures.

She thought she looked swollen, like she was retaining water, like she was sickly.

That same week had the man reconsidering his career path. He looked into podiatry, dental supplies.

Neither was sure how to conduct themselves over dinner. They were both uneasy and unaccustomed to dining with another person. There was wine, appetizers, salads, entrées, dessert, premature emissions. Otherwise, it was dim sum or tapas, something light. It was so long ago neither can quite remember. There was only casual mention of the minor procedure, of the career path. Neither pressed the other for details as neither seemed eager to disclose certain matters. It was early and inappropriate. Both noted each other's height. She was a good head taller than he. Both decided it meant nothing, this particular difference. However, they each understood that nothing is relative to both something and everything and situated in close proximity to neither. There is a continuum and they both were aware of this.

They engaged in the standard back and forth with the understanding that standard back and forth is neither standard nor back and forth.

The woman says, Surely there has to be…
The man says, I couldn't agree more.
This went on for weeks, these dinners, conversations.

Then they went to bed, all arms and legs. There was awkwardness, confusion, frustration.

This, too, went on for weeks.

She says, This is why I married you.
He says, Because I've never thought to have sexual intercourse with an automobile.

She says, And you're good around the house.

He says, I am versatile. She says, If nothing else.

He says, It's my versatility that's gotten me where I am today.

She says, You are a dangerous man.

He says, Hide the women and children.

She says, And the Buicks.

He says, I don't think I shall ever see...

She says, My only husband fuck a tree.

He is funny when he calls himself versatile. He is not at all versatile, nor is he good around the house. The man doesn't know how to do anything, but he tries and what this means is he will go through the motions until it appears he has exhausted every option. Then he calls his friend to come over and has him perform the household tasks and repairs that he has failed to complete.

His friend has installed the new toilet, the toilet seat, assembled the bookcase in the living room, installed air conditioners.

The friend fixed the shower door when it went off track last year. He also recalibrated the faucet so that the hot water lined up with the red indicator. For years it had been off some forty degrees.

Forty degrees as a measurement of angle, not temperature.

Although the hot water has never been very hot.

He finished the job by testing the shower himself, unbeknownst to the woman, who walked in on him soaping his abdomen.

They both apologized to each other, though neither was sincere.

Both told the story to the man, who thought nothing of it.

The woman said, What kind of person showers at someone else's house. She called the friend names when she told the story to the man.

The man tried to think of an answer but came up empty.

The man and woman have never showered together, not even in the beginning of their courtship.

Both think bathing is a private matter.

Ancient Greeks utilized small bathtubs, wash basins, and foot baths for personal cleanliness. The earliest findings of baths date from the mid-second millennium BCE in the palace complex at Knossos, Crete, and the luxurious alabaster bathtubs excavated in Akrotiri, Santorini. The Greeks established public baths and showers within gymnasiums for relaxation and personal hygiene. The word *gymnasium* comes from the Greek word *gymnos*, meaning naked.

The man and woman ignored the many red flags out of foolishness or hopefulness.

Hope is always foolish and fools are always hopeful.

Surely someone, a poet or philosopher, has said this before.

They were both eager to get on with their lives. They were eager to live like adults. As such, they committed to grand plans and carried the plans out in secret. They didn't want to include any friends or family. This decision seems indicative of something, but it's unclear what. They've never been able to draw any conclusions concerning this decision. For years, it bothered both of them. What bothered them most was that the other seemed so eager to go along with the idea of excluding everyone from their plans.

Certainly there was an ordained minister, a witness, and a room for the night.

The witness was bought and paid for, part of the deal.

There was a mutual decision to forego the threshold ceremony. The man wasn't big enough or strong enough to pick up and carry the woman. It is possible that the woman might've been capable of doing this, but neither wanted to confront such a thing at the time. It was only years later that they felt comfortable performing their trick at parties.

The woman would rest her chin on the top of the man's head and they'd affect certain expressions to induce laughter.

The man has never been strong. As a boy he was never able to do any pushups or pull-ups in gym class.

Fools rush in where angels fear to tread was first written by Alexander Pope, in his poem "An Essay on Criticism," in 1711.

Alexander Pope was a dwarf, so almost anyone could rest his or her chin on top of his head.

The woman spent an inordinate amount of time in the bathroom reflecting in the mirror above the sink. It might've felt like five minutes or months or years. The man examined his genitals under the covers while she was in the bathroom. He made sure to wash himself thoroughly before the ceremony. He's always been hypervigilant when it comes to hygiene, as has the woman.

Certainly the requisite goings-on ensued, pushing and pulling, testing and retesting, all arms and legs.

Awkwardness, confusion, frustration.

The man says, Joyce fucking Kilmer. Tree-fucking dendrophiliac.
The woman says, Every day was Arbor Day for him.

There is quiet. They sip at coffee, bite into pastries.

The woman says, Certainly lightning can take down a tree. A hurricane.
The man says, But can a tree fall of natural causes?
The woman says, Those are natural causes.
The man says, Termites are natural causes.
The woman says, Women are natural causes.
The man says, Same difference.
The woman says, Or vice versa.

Outside neighbors pass as they walk a dog. These are neighbors from down the block. The woman is friendly with both and sees them around town. They, too, are a married couple. Almost all of the neighbors on this block are married.

This couple is roughly the same age as the principals, as are most of the neighbors, save one or two nearing retirement.

This couple, the one walking the dog, live their own lives and have almost nothing to do with the principals, except for certain community endeavors. Along with the woman, they were part of the crew that cleaned the park after the latest hurricane. Trees had been damaged and branches were scattered everywhere and it was dangerous. Children could get hurt, as could any of the feeble-minded adults that live in the area.

The neighborhood features a home for feeble-minded adults. They are often seen walking through the park in teams before settling onto the great lawn to play games of kickball.

The hurricane uprooted any number of trees in the park and the streets surrounding the park. This was unusual but not unexpected. Every so often hurricanes pass through this part of the country, but it seems to be happening at a greater frequency the last few years.

This was a time during global warming, which was a hot-button issue for decades.

The woman took pictures of the uprooted trees and showed them to the man. She took pictures of the holes under the trees, which looked like portals into an underground world. They talked about Mother Nature's power and fury and how small it made them feel.

The woman talked about the environment and things that could be done to prevent the world's destruction.

They discussed this at the kitchen table on a Sunday morning over coffee and pastries while reading the newspaper.

This day they are discussing other matters.

Outside there is a world in motion involving people and dogs and trees and birds. The sky and sun are out there, too.

There are no hurricanes on the horizon, though a tropical depression is beginning to form in the Caribbean.

This depression could turn into a hurricane but it is too soon to tell.

Hurricanes evolve through a life cycle of stages from birth to death. A tropical disturbance in time can grow to a more intense stage by attaining a specified wind speed.

Hurricanes can often live for a long period of time, as much as two to three weeks. They may initiate as a cluster of thunderstorms over tropical ocean waters. Once a disturbance has become a tropical depression, the amount of time it takes to achieve the next stage, tropical storm, can take anywhere from half a day to as much as two days. It may not happen at all. The same may occur for the amount of time a tropical storm needs to intensify into a hurricane. Atmospheric and oceanic conditions play major roles in determining these events.

Should this depression turn into a hurricane its name will be Melissa, as Melissa is next on the list.

Hurricanes used to be designated by a system of latitude-longitude, which was an easy way for meteorologists to track them. However, once the public began receiving storm warnings, this became confusing. Scientific precision was discarded in favor of a system of names.

In 1953, the National Weather Service picked up on the habit of Naval meteorologists of naming the storms after women. Ships were always referred to as female, and were often given women's names. In 1979, male names began to alternate with the female names.

There are actually six lists of names in use for storms in the Atlantic. These lists rotate, one each year; the list of this year's names will not be reused for six years. The names get recycled each time the list comes up, with one exception: storms so devastating that reusing the name is inappropriate. In this case, the name is taken off the list and another name is used to replace it.

The man says, Vice versa. Vicey versey. Is that Latin?
The woman says, I don't know Latin.
The man says, Me neither.

The woman says, Does anyone?
The man says, Does anyone what?
The woman says, I don't remember.

Outside, on the driveway, a pair of slugs is making their way from one end to another. This journey takes five minutes or days or months. They leave a visible trail behind them and as such are easy to track. However, the two slugs will go unnoticed this day. They will make it safely to wherever it is they're going.

The slugs are apropos of nothing, but they are out there.

The man has poured salt on countless slugs over the years and has left their desiccated carcasses out on the driveway as a warning to others.

The man doesn't need his friend to do everything.

He says, Your friend.
She says, Does anyone remember my friend?
He says, I don't. What I mean is, I can't remember…
She says, You shouldn't remember her.
He says, Why not?
She says, She is not memorable.
He says, I think I loved her once.
She says, I think you're mistaken. I think you're thinking of someone else.
He says, You are probably right.

There is no telling what the man is referring to here.

Maybe three weeks after the wedding, the woman died in her sleep but was resurrected by the man. This is how he thinks of it, though it was clearly resuscitation and not resurrection.

The man is not at all religious and neither is the woman.

He didn't think he was capable of resuscitating anybody, as such a thing takes knowhow and skill. The man had never taken a class on CPR but had seen CPR performed on television and so he went through those particular motions. First he tried clearing her airway, which was already clear, and then he blew into her mouth. In between these breaths, he pounded on her chest. He counted to five while doing the chest compressions.

Cardiopulmonary resuscitation (CPR) is an emergency procedure, performed in an effort to manually preserve intact brain function until further measures are taken to restore spontaneous blood circulation and breathing in a person in cardiac arrest. It is indicated in those who are unresponsive with no breathing or abnormal breathing; for example, agonal respirations.

What happened was she stopped breathing in the middle of the night. She'd told him when they first started sleeping together that she had a sleep disorder, which meant he shouldn't be alarmed should she wake with a start in the middle of the night. He also shouldn't be alarmed should she fly out of bed and run around the bedroom or climb out a window.

So the man was prepared for something to happen in the middle of the night.

This particular episode happened at his father's house. It is apropos of something, but nothing specific and nothing anyone can identify.

Everything open to interpretation and misinterpretation.

After a minute or so, the woman came to. The man wasn't sure how to conduct himself. He thought it appropriate to give her some air, give her time, room. He asked if he should call for an ambulance and she said no. She said this had happened before, that it was likely to happen again.

CPR alone is unlikely to restart the heart; its main purpose is to restore partial flow of oxygenated blood to the brain and heart. The objective is to delay tissue death and to extend the brief window of opportunity for a successful resuscitation without permanent brain damage.

She said she was fine. She said she was used to it.
He said, You stopped breathing.
She said, But I started back up.
He said, Only after I saved you.
She said, Thanks for that.
He said, You're welcome.
She said, I would've started breathing on my own before long. Just so you know.

The man decided not to respond to this last statement. The man wasn't sure what to think.

The woman has stopped breathing in the middle of the night several times since and has always started back up again on her own.

In the nineteenth century, Doctor H. R. Silvester described a method of artificial respiration in which the patient is laid on their back, their arms raised above their head to aid inhalation and then pressed against their chest to aid exhalation. The procedure is repeated sixteen times per minute. This type of artificial respiration is occasionally seen in films made in the early part of the twentieth century and is probably the first recorded description of formal resuscitation.

The man might be referring to the woman he was involved with before he met the woman he was to marry at the going away party.

The woman he was involved with was the woman going away. This woman was leaving in the morning. She was going overseas, back to where she'd come from, where she was raised. She would probably return in a year or two. She was hoping to maybe pick her life back up where she was leaving it off, leaving it behind.

It's unclear if the man was part of what she wanted to pick up again.

This woman wasn't going away specifically to leave the man behind. In fact, she said she was sorry for that part of it. She said it was regrettable. She said she had business to take care of back home. It was a great opportunity, one she couldn't pass up.

The man and woman are reading. They are across from each other at the kitchen table.

The man rises and walks to the counter where the coffee pot sits. There is still at least half a pot of coffee remaining. Soon someone will have to make another pot. For the sake of fair play, let's say they take turns doing this. The house rule is, whoever finishes a pot is responsible for starting the next one. The man and woman can drink up to three pots of coffee on a Sunday between the two of them.

The man refills his cup and asks his wife if she'd like a refill. More often than not, she will want a refill, but not always. Sometimes he will refill her cup without asking but sometimes she scolds him for this. She'll say something like, Who said I wanted more coffee.

At first she doesn't respond because she is concentrating on the story she is reading, which concerns the city council and their efforts to shut down a local massage parlor.

He says, I remember loving her once.
She says, When do you remember loving her?

He says, It was summer, I think, and the city was empty. Everyone was somewhere else. When I say everyone, I mean everyone I knew. There were other people, sure, but I did not know them. I didn't care to know them. I saw them milling about on the street, congregating in barrooms and restaurants, but I had nothing to do with those people. They had their own lives to tend to and I couldn't be bothered. And the truth is those people wanted nothing to do with me either. It was all very mutual.

She says, They were fall-down trees in a fall-down forest.

He says, Indeed. I remember having nothing to do at all. I remember every day there was nothing. There was no one to visit, no one to drink with, nothing to work on, nothing going on whatsoever.

She says, Where was I during this?

He says, I don't remember, where were you?

She says, Were we together then?

He says, This is what I don't know. I remember I spent most of my time waiting for the mail. Every day I waited for the mailman to deliver the mail. Every day I looked out the window and kept watch for him. Had I a candle I would've put it in the window. I think his name was Benjamin. I think he was like a father to me.

It probably wouldn't surprise anyone that the woman developed asthma shortly after the resuscitation. The man would listen to her wheeze in the middle of the night. He'd say, Isn't this why you have an inhaler?

She wouldn't respond to this question.

She's never wanted to acknowledge that she has asthma, that she is the sort of person who'd develop asthma.

It would be the same if she had diabetes, which she doesn't have.

Someday, though, she might develop diabetes.

She hasn't exercised at all since the marriage started.

Asthma was recognized in Ancient Egypt and was treated by drinking an incense mixture known as kyphi. Hippocrates officially named it as a respiratory problem circa 450 BCE, with the Greek word for "panting" forming the basis of our modern name. During the 1930s to 1950s, asthma was known as one of the "holy seven" psychosomatic illnesses. Its cause was considered psychological, with treatment often based on psychoanalysis and other talking cures. These psychoanalysts interpreted the asthmatic wheeze as the suppressed cry of the child for its mother, and considered the treatment of depression to be especially important for individuals with asthma.

Which isn't to say the woman suffers from depression, or has suffered from depression.

But it's likely she's had bouts of depression all her adult life.

This memory of summer, of the city empty, of everyone somewhere else, others milling about and congregating in barrooms, and this love of someone, is not at all accurate. It's an amalgam of various memories from different times and places.

The man doesn't even believe what it is he's saying about loving this friend.

When he was a boy there was a mailman named Ben. Everyone called this mailman Ben. His father called him Ben, as did all the neighbors. No one ever called him Benjamin.

Ben was a mailman to the boy. They had no connection beyond that.

Perhaps there was a brief exchange on the weather or baseball.

The boy could be seen playing baseball across the street from his house, where Ben would deliver mail. The boy would either play with the neighborhood boys or his father.

His father played baseball with him from the time he could stand up on his own. His father was a gifted athlete and thought the same would hold true for his son.

The same did hold true for his son. The boy was also a gifted athlete, though he was never physically strong. He could never do a push up or pull up, but he could hit and throw and run and jump and do extraordinary things on the fields and courts all over the county.

There were hopes of turning pro one day, or at least a scholarship.

His father cautioned against this sort of hope.

He cited any number of statistics and relayed anecdotes, cited precedents.

His father advised the son to fix the hitch in his swing, for instance.

He said one can't catch up to a major league fastball with a pronounced hitch.

The woman says, And your own father? What was he?
The man says, He was in and out.
The woman says, I'm sure he was.
The man says, He was busy working. He wasn't around much.
The woman says, Missing in action.
The man says, He was a good father.

The woman says, Loved by one and all.

The man says, What are we talking about?

The woman says, Maybe you should call and ask him. Your father. He is probably home now, wandering the halls reciting.... What does he recite again?

The man says, Aristophanes.

The woman says, I thought it was Euripides.

The man says, What's the difference?

The woman says, Vive le difference.

The man says, Why should I call him?

The woman looks at the man. It seems as if she wants to say something. There is a particular look on her face.

She is squinting ever so slightly. This squint is hardly perceptible.

The man recognizes this squint, but no one else would.

It's as if she is thinking about what she wants to say, like she is organizing her thoughts, assembling the appropriate syntax and diction.

The man waits for her to say something.

It goes on like this for a while.

She thinks better of it, decides it will keep.

It's unclear what's on her mind.

Outside the slugs are still on the driveway, leaving an easy-to-follow trail behind them, still on their way elsewhere, still slugging it out.

The neighbors with the dog are no longer out there. They have concluded their walk, which they take every Sunday without fail, rain or shine. They do this for an hour, sometimes even longer.

The man sees them from inside his own kitchen. If he is outside on the driveway pouring salt on slugs, he will wave. If one or the other says hello he will say hello back. He might even say, How are you today or Good to see you.

He has never engaged either of these neighbors in any kind of conversation.

There's no way of knowing what the neighbors with the dog are doing now that they have returned home. Perhaps they're not even home. Perhaps they are out and about in the world at large doing what people do on Sunday mornings. They could be shopping or going for a drive in the country.

They could be Sunday drivers, which is a term the man doesn't hear anymore.

He remembers his father saying this many times. Goddamned Sunday drivers was how he always put it.

The man's father does recite poetry from time to time, but never classical playwrights like Aristophanes or Euripides.

The man and woman have lived in this house for years now. It is the only home they've ever lived in together.

The house is a Cape Cod cottage, which is a style of house originating in New England in the seventeenth century. It is traditionally characterized by a low, broad frame building, generally a story and a half high, with a steep, pitched roof with end gables, a large central chimney, and little ornamentation.

Traditional Cape Cod houses are simple, symmetrically designed with a central front door surrounded by two multi-paned windows on each side. Homes were designed to withstand the stormy, stark weather of the Massachusetts coast.

This is the house they live in.

Looking for this house proved difficult and quite a process. It took six months altogether, but it seemed like years. They could never agree on certain particulars—city or suburban living, apartment or house, neighborhoods, amenities.

There was awkwardness, confusion, frustration.

They'd made an offer on another house before finding the Cape Cod, one that was out of their price range.

This house was not a Cape Cod, but rather a Colonial.

These buildings typically included steep roofs, small casement windows due to a scarcity of glass in the Colonies, rich ornamentation, and a massive central chimney. To maximize natural light in northern climes, early houses faced southeast, regardless of a building's alignment to the road. Conversely, in southern colonies, houses faced northwest to minimize the sun's heat.

Essentially the Colonial was bigger. Also, there were multiple levels, small staircases that included only a few steps in either direction. There were also built-in bookshelves.

This is what they remember of the Colonial.

They were desperate and tired of looking and tried to justify this potential expenditure in various ways. One was that it seemed a good investment and that, if worse went down to worst, they would get their money back. Still, they didn't like the idea of overextending themselves.

But they were also tired of looking.

Their offer was considerably lower than the asking price. There was at the same time another offer on the table, though they didn't know for what amount.

They assumed the other offer was higher than theirs.

They were advised by the realtor to write a letter to the owners explaining why they loved the house and how they would be the best possible new owners for it. They were told to detail their personal histories, highlighting where they'd come from and what they hoped to achieve in the future and what they loved about the house, which seemed as if it were built for them, as if it were a dream house.

All of this seemed futile at the time, as it does in retrospect.

Of course, the other offer was accepted and they had to keep looking.

They looked every weekend. They kept in close touch with the realtor, who told them not to be discouraged. She relayed statistics, anecdotes, cited precedents.

Finally they found and decided on the Cape Cod.

How they decided was the woman said I like it and the man said Finally.

That other house, the one they'd made the low-ball offer on and had written a letter to the owners highlighting their histories and hopes, was actually a Ranch.

For some reason they both remember it as a Colonial.

The man sometimes refers to his own house, the Cape Cod, as the domicile.

He'll be out with his friend at a bar or restaurant or in the park and he'll say, Let's go back to the domicile.

The friend is coming over later and might stay for dinner.

This is likely to be a problem.

The domicile is not located on the Massachusetts coast, but it is often in the path of hurricanes and otherwise stark, stormy weather.

The domicile is green inside, different shades of green.

Eleven of Aristophanes' thirty plays survive virtually complete. These, together with fragments of some of his other plays, provide the only real examples of a genre of comic drama known as Old Comedy, and they are used to define the genre. Aristophanes has been said to recreate the life of ancient Athens more convincingly than any other author.

His powers of ridicule were feared and acknowledged by influential contemporaries; Plato singled out Aristophanes' play *The Clouds* as slander that contributed to the trial and subsequent execution of Socrates, although other satirical playwrights had also caricatured the philosopher.

In his time, Euripides was associated with Socrates as a leader of a decadent intellectualism, both of them being frequently lampooned by comic poets such as Aristophanes. Whereas Socrates was eventually put on trial and executed as a corrupting influence, Euripides chose a voluntary exile in old age, dying in Macedonia.

Some ancient scholars attributed ninety-five plays to him, but according to the Suda, it was ninety-two at most. Of these, eighteen or nineteen have survived more or less complete. There are also fragments, some substantial, of most of the other plays.

More of his plays have survived intact than those of Aeschylus and Sophocles together, partly due to chance and partly because his popularity grew as theirs declined.

However, Aeschylus and Sophocles aren't currently under discussion, nor are they likely to come up later.

The Suda or Souda is a massive tenth-century Byzantine encyclopedia of the ancient Mediterranean world, formerly attributed to an author called Suidas. It is an encyclopedic lexicon, written in Greek, with thirty thousand entries, many drawing from ancient sources that have since been lost, and often derived from medieval Christian compilers.

The man and woman painted the interior of the house themselves. The man was responsible for the dining room and kitchen, while the woman took care of the living room and den.

It's more accurate to say the man and woman painted the downstairs of the house themselves. After accomplishing this, they decided to hire professionals to paint the rest of the interior, including the stairwell and the two bedrooms upstairs.

The man did a shoddy job of painting the dining room and kitchen, in particular along the molding. He wasn't adept at taping, nor did he take the time to use a smaller brush for the more delicate work.

There are blotches of green paint along the ceilings in both rooms. Some are larger than others, though most go unnoticed.

The woman noticed these blotches straight away. She considered pointing out the man's mistakes. She considered showing exactly what he did wrong and how he could correct it, how he could do better next time.

Ultimately, she decided to say nothing. She decided to keep it to herself. She figured the man did his best.

Eventually she did say something about the blotches. This was maybe a week or two later, at the dinner table.

The dinner table is the same as the breakfast table.

It is the kitchen table, the one they are currently sitting at, the one that has coffee mugs and pastries sitting atop it, along with the newspaper.

They were eating takeout Chinese food. It has been their practice to eat takeout Chinese food once a week.

They order from one of two places. This decision is made together and they discuss it beforehand. One person will not unilaterally decide from which Chinese takeout place they should order on a particular night.

The difference between the two Chinese takeout restaurants is marginal. One has better dumplings, the other better fried rice.

Although, this is entirely subjective. There is another couple in the neighborhood that believes the opposite regarding the dumplings and fried rice.

The rest of the respective menus is almost indistinguishable.

The man asked the woman to pass the lo mein.

She said, Even a child could do better, as she passed the lo mein to her husband.

The man wasn't sure what she was referring to and didn't ask, but it turns out it was the paint job.

He says, At any rate. Every day I would wait for the mail and occupy myself with minutia.
She says, This is our national occupation. Minutia.
He says, There's no point arguing.

This is something the man says out loud from time to time, but he doesn't believe it. He enjoys arguing, as it presents an opportunity to learn something. This is what he tells himself, what he tells his wife.

But it's also an opportunity for him to demonstrate a certain learned proficiency in any number of disciplines and subjects.

The man enjoys learning but forgets most of what he learns.

The man will spend hours on the Internet looking up information on any number of subjects. He is most interested in historical figures and weather and sports and aberrant sexual behaviors.

He can spend hours looking up encyclopedia entries, getting lost in all the information, this factoid concerning geology sparking curiosity in that factoid about space-time and so forth.

Thus, he can never retain what he's read, what he's tried to learn.

Still, this is one of his favorite pastimes, this futile pursuit of the arcane and trivial.

He cannot bring himself to reference the source of this information in conversation, as he finds the name too ridiculous to mention, a cross between a cartoon-character and a fatal disease.

The woman knows this full well and allows the man to indulge in these conversations more often than not.

Of course, the man cannot recall what minutia occupied him during the time he is discussing; such is the nature of minutia.

The woman almost comments on the nature of minutia and how this is everything we do in the world, everything there is. She catches herself, and is pleased to have done so.

After the professional painters painted the rest of the house, the man and woman adopted a dog from the local shelter.

It wasn't immediately after the painters finished painting.

There was an interval.

It wasn't as if the painters had just pulled out of the driveway, had just packed up all of the tarps, stood back and admired their work, called the owners over to discuss the billing options and said their goodbyes, and the man and woman rushed off to the shelter to adopt a dog.

It wasn't as if the paint had yet to dry.

But sometime after the painters finished painting, the man and woman adopted a dog from the local shelter.

It is safe to assume nothing of note happened during this interval.

The man and woman did sleep in a hotel for a week, though, waiting for the paint to dry.

At the same time, they were waiting for the floor to finish drying, too.

At the same time they had the place painted, they had the floors refinished.

The woman said, This house is toxic and we can't stay here.

She didn't cite her asthma or any respiratory difficulties as the reason for leaving, but it was clearly the reason.

The woman had always wanted a dog of her own, as she was denied one growing up due to her mother's allergies.

It's not clear if her mother ever had an actual physical allergy to dogs.

They drove to the shelter on a Saturday. They had settled into their new house and it was no longer toxic. Perhaps there was a slight hint of wax or turpentine or paint thinner or finish. The man's eyes did burn for a while, but he kept this to himself.

The weather was perfect and not at all stormy or stark. Perfect conditions for picking out a dog and taking that dog for a walk, which was the plan.

They moved up and down the room that housed all of the dogs. The dogs were behind cages, locked up. They looked like prisoners.

The woman said, Doesn't this break your heart.
The man said, I know.

The man's heart wasn't broken or in the process of breaking during this time.

These dogs had been abandoned or abused by their previous owners. These were rescued dogs. As such, most of these dogs looked skittish and of poor disposition.

The man said, I'm not sure about this.
The woman said, What aren't you sure of?
The man said, These dogs look skittish. They look of poor disposition.
The woman said, They've been abused.
The man said, I can tell.
The woman said, Well, I'm sure of this. This is something I'm sure of. These dogs need loving homes and I'm sure that we're adopting a dog today.

They settled on a small but athletic-looking mutt, a female. She had light eyes and seemed to be the most docile of the group.

They named her Georgia for no particular reason.

Actually, there was a reason they named her Georgia, but they both have forgotten.

In this context, Georgia doesn't refer to the U.S. state, nor does it refer to the country in the Caucasus region of Eurasia. It comes from a series of children's books the man has never read, which is but one in a long list of books the man has never read.

The country Georgia is located at the crossroads of Western Asia and Eastern Europe. It is bounded to the west by the Black Sea, to the north by Russia, to the south by Turkey and Armenia, and to the southeast by Azerbaijan. The capital and largest city is Tbilisi.

The state Georgia was established in 1732, the last of the original Thirteen Colonies. Named after King George II of Great Britain, Georgia was the fourth state to ratify the United States Constitution, on January 2, 1788. It declared its secession from the Union on January 19, 1861, and was one of the original seven Confederate states. It was the last state to be restored to the Union, on July 15, 1870.

The man and woman have been to neither Georgia nor Georgia.

The woman says, This morning I was in bed....
The man says, I'm sorry...
The woman says, I said this morning I was in bed.
The man says, Weren't we discussing something?
The woman says, When?
The man says, Just now.
The woman says, I thought we were finished.
The man says, Were we?
The woman says, I think so.
The man says, You are probably right.
It is quiet. Neither sips at coffee or bites into a pastry.
They look at each other, past or through.
The man says, So, this morning you were in bed....
She says, That's right. This morning I was in bed and I saw seagulls flying aimlessly out the window. Against the blue backdrop of the sky. It was nice.

He says, Was I still sleeping?

She says, I think you were downstairs already.

He says, Okay. So it was nice…

She says, It was nice. Every few seconds I'd lose sight of them—they were flying in and out of sight. Sometimes they were flying…I mean, I saw them flapping their wings…and sometimes they floated.

He says, They are nasty creatures. Filthy.

She says, What were you waiting for?

He says, When?

She says, When you were waiting for the mail. Were you expecting a package, a letter, a check?

He says, That's a good question. Perhaps it was a letter. Perhaps I was waiting for a letter from you. Maybe you were overseas and I was pining.

It should come as no surprise that the man didn't adjust to having a dog in the house. The dog displayed any number of peculiar behaviors, not the least of which was extraordinary hyperactivity. The man speculated that along with being traumatized from whatever abuse she'd suffered, the dog had some kind of glandular issue, something hormonal. The dog couldn't seem to calm down at all.

The dog was always running around and barking and clawing and biting and chewing on everything in the house. The dog was manic, troubled.

Finally the man couldn't take it anymore.

He said to his wife, I can't take this dog anymore.

The woman said, I know.

The truth is the woman didn't adjust well to the dog, either. She had more patience for the dog than the man, understood what the dog had been through, but she also understood that there was something very wrong with this dog.

She said, I don't think this is the kind of dog that people who've never had a dog should have for their first dog.
He said, Let's get rid of her.

They discussed how they should get rid of the dog.

The man didn't say out loud that he could drive the dog over to the woods and turn her loose. He knew this wouldn't be received well. He knew it would make him sound cruel and inhumane.

It was decided they would find someone to readopt the dog.

They decided in conjunction with this first decision that they couldn't return the dog to the shelter. They couldn't say there was something wrong with the dog, that they'd changed their minds.

The woman is the one who made these decisions. The man indicated his approval by saying yes from time to time and nodding his head.

The woman decided to bequeath the dog to a colleague. The woman was both frank and forthright about the dog's behavioral issues, but the colleague told her it shouldn't be a problem.

Shortly thereafter the colleague found another job and was no longer a colleague. They never heard about Georgia again.

Maybe once or twice the woman said out loud that she wondered whatever became of Georgia.

The man never once wondered this.

The woman has never been overseas and the man was never pining for her.

The woman has never left the continent.

She has a passport but has never used it. The passport is now expired and sits under other documents and papers in a file cabinet.

Still, she'd like to travel someday. There is a host of countries she'd like to visit.

Europe she's especially interested in.

Particularly Italy, Spain, Portugal, England, France.

She has no interest, however, in visiting Austria, Germany, Switzerland, and the whole of Eastern Europe, Georgia included.

Nor is she interested in Asia or South America.

There are reasons for this, having to do with history and art and architecture and language and culture.

The reasons have nothing to do with heritage or ethnicity. There is no personal history, prompting these interests. The woman does have a history with seagulls.

Once she found an injured seagull on the street. The seagull's left leg had been damaged. It looked like the seagull had gotten into a street fight and lost, like another animal had taken umbrage, liberties.

She collected the seagull and placed it in a box and brought it home with her.

This was before she met the man, before the going away party, before all of it.

She crumbled some white bread and dropped it into the box that night to feed the seagull.

She didn't know what seagulls ate, but she'd seen them eat white bread on beaches.

She'd seen people throw pieces of white bread at the seagulls.

She suspected they ate fish, but she didn't have any fish, not even a can of tuna. And she was too tired to go out to buy a can of tuna for a seagull.

The next day she brought the seagull to an animal hospital. She asked them what they were going to do for the seagull and they said they'd take care of it.

She understood what this meant, the subtext.

She says, I think you are referring to your father's cabin upstate. I used to go to your father's cabin upstate sometimes, which isn't overseas. There I could be alone and enjoy nature.

He says, Nature can kill you.
She says, Anything can kill you.
He says, It's not safe out there, that much is certain.

The newspaper today has people being killed in factory fires, explosions, shootouts, car accidents, bicycle accidents, train accidents, other kinds of accidents, hurricanes, tornadoes, earthquakes, tsunamis, floods, droughts, domestic disputes, desert warfare, guerrilla warfare, police brutality, acts of genocide, acts of terrorism.

She says, I almost always enjoyed your father's cabin upstate, except for that one time when he was there.

He says, I don't remember, where was I?

She says, You were here pining, apparently.

He says, Yes, while you were overseas at the cabin living it up with Mother Nature.

She says, I have never been overseas without you. I have never been overseas with you, either. You and I have not left the continent. We are bound to it.

He says, We are bound to each other.

She says, Mortally bound.

He says, What happened with my father and the cabin?

She says, I saw him there once.

He says, And?

She says, after pausing, I wasn't expecting him.

He says, And what do you mean with the seagulls?

She says, I don't mean anything with the seagulls.

He says, This is hard to follow.

She says, Not for the rest of us.

This is probably not hard to follow, this particular conversation between these particular people.

A monkey can probably follow this.

Which isn't to say that if one cannot follow this particular conversation that one is somehow less than a monkey.

The man wants to reference something called *The Seagull*, but he isn't sure what it is, so he says nothing. He thinks it either a movie or play, perhaps one performed in the park. He vaguely remembers the woman suggesting they go see a play in the park, but they'd have to wake up early and wait in line for tickets, which is something the man has no interest in.

The man has always enjoyed reading into certain parts of conversation, interpreting the subtext. He enjoys trying to read body language. He is not as good at this as he thinks.

This is why he says this is hard to follow. Sometimes he wants things spelled out plain and to the purpose.

He says, And all of this means what?
She says, I don't know what you're talking about.
He says, There isn't some kind of double meaning here?
She says, What kind of double meaning? With the seagulls?
He says, With the seagulls, with my father…
She says, No.
He says, Filthy rotten seagulls flying and floating out of view and I'm downstairs all the while. Also out of view.
She says, You called the seagulls filthy and rotten.
He says, Everyone knows seagulls are filthy and rotten.

Most everyone does, in fact, know that seagulls are filthy and rotten.

Seagulls scavenge and beg for food, like vultures and dogs. They nest in large, densely packed, noisy colonies. The sounds they make, the squawks, are decidedly unpleasant. Some gull colonies display mobbing behavior, attacking and harassing would-be predators or intruders, and even innocent bystanders from time to time. They even kill their own—and for what, is what the man would like to know.

Monkeys are worse.

She says, I once rescued a seagull.

He says, Rescued it from what?

She says, It was hurt. I came home late one night and saw a seagull limping across the street. I thought a car was going to run him over, so I scooped him up and put him in my bag and took him home.

He says, Did he sleep with you?

She says, I put him in a box. He was nice.

The man decides to say nothing about this. He decides this is none of his business.

The man cannot understand how a seagull can be nice.

Sometimes he cannot understand the woman he married.

The Seagull is a play by Russian dramatist and writer Anton Chekhov, written in 1895 and first produced in 1896.

The opening night of the first production was an abject failure. Vera Komissarzhevskaya, playing Nina, was so intimidated by the hostility of the audience that she lost her voice.

Chekhov left his seat in the theater and spent the last two acts behind the scenes.

However, when Constantin Stanislavski, the seminal Russian theater practitioner of the time, directed it in 1898 for his Moscow Art Theatre, the play was a triumph.

Stanislavski's production of *The Seagull* became one of the greatest events in the history of Russian and world theater.

The woman didn't give up on the idea of owning a dog. However many months after they got rid of Georgia, she decided that a pure-bred dog was a better idea. She said it would be easier to handle than a rescue dog. She said purebreds were less likely to be manic or have glandular issues.

When she was a child her grandmother had a standard poodle named Blackie. This was the dog she wanted, a black standard poodle.

The poodle is believed to have originated in Germany, dating back to the fifteenth century. Poodles are retrievers or gun dogs and are still used by hunters in that role. Their coats are moisture-resistant, which helps their swimming.

The poodle is an active, intelligent, and elegant dog, squarely built and well proportioned. To ensure the desirable squarely built appearance, the length of body measured from the breastbone to the point of the rump approximates the height from the highest point of the shoulders to the ground. The eyes are generally dark, oval in shape, and have an alert and intelligent expression. The ears fold over close to the head, set at, or slightly below, eye level. The coat is a naturally curly texture, dense throughout, although most registered show dogs have a lion cut or other, similarly shaven look.

The woman researched breeders that featured a natural and holistic approach to raising dogs and found one several states away.

This after investigating countless breeders from all over the country.

The dog was going to cost over a thousand dollars.

The dog was going to be an investment.

But they were desperate and tired of looking and tried to justify this potential expenditure in various ways. One was that it seemed a good investment and that, if worse went down to worst, they could sell the dog on the Internet or the man could drive it to the woods and turn it loose.

Still, the man was leery of overextending themselves.

He said, Isn't that a lot for a dog.
She said, It's the going rate.

Later that night, after dinner, she said, This is what happens when you can't handle a rescue dog.

The last thing the man had said concerned the local football team.

They set out early the next morning. The man is always insistent upon starting trips as early as possible. The man cannot abide traffic.

The woman had mapped out a route and made reservations for a hotel so they could spend the night, as the breeder was several states away.

The hotel was just off the interstate, approximately halfway between home and the breeder's. There were two queen-sized beds in the room and as they got undressed and ready to retire for the evening, the woman asked which bed the man wanted.

He said, Excuse me?
She said, Which bed do you want?
He said, Which bed do you want?
She said, It doesn't matter to me.

He said, We're not sleeping in the same bed?
She said, We sleep in the same bed every night.

That night, while under the covers, the man masturbated in protest.

He started off doing this quietly but decided not to hold back as he continued. The woman slept through it and the rest of the night without stirring.

It's possible she did hear her husband masturbating.

Sometimes the man starts masturbating when they are in bed with each other. It's a kind of foreplay.

He hopes the woman will become aroused and lend aid and comfort.

He hopes this will provoke her into passion.

This has happened more than once, actually.

Most recently, though, she asked, Does that feel good?
He said, It does.

She didn't say anything after that.

They started off early again the next morning and made it to the breeder's before noon.

After the requisite amenities, they were escorted to where the puppies were being held.

On the way to this room, they walked past any number of dogs behind cages. They looked like prisoners.

The man and woman moved up and down the room, inspecting the various poodles. They'd been informed six weeks ago that an apricot poodle was about to give birth, so that was the color they were getting.

The woman had wanted a black standard but settled for apricot. The man actually preferred the apricot, for no particular reason.

Let's say for now the dog is apricot, but later he can be black or white or some other color altogether.

The puppies were all turned loose in a big room. The woman was delighted.

The man looked over to his wife and saw her delighted. He liked to see her like this.

After a certain amount of deliberation, they decided on the one that seemed to take to them the most. This puppy immediately ran over to the both of them and acted as all puppies act.

All of the dogs seemed energetic and this concerned the man. But the woman told him that all puppies are energetic and this will last only a couple of years. She also said they spend most of the day and night sleeping. She said it was going to be much easier this time around.

The woman sat in the backseat and cradled their new puppy on the drive back to the hotel. Every so often the man would check the rearview mirror to look at them together.

That night the man and woman slept in the same bed, along with the dog.

The man didn't realize the dog was going to sleep with them.

The woman said, It will only be for the first few nights, so he doesn't feel alone.

After a long pause, the man said, Okay.

The man is still thinking about the injured seagull. He doesn't want to but he can't help himself.

The woman thinks nothing of it. She doesn't think it unusual for someone to care about animals, all kinds of animals.

The man says, I was thinking about dinner last night. At the restaurant.

The woman says, What about it?

The man says, It reminded me of something, but I can't remember what.

The woman says, Then my guess is it didn't remind you of anything. It was new.

The man says, We've been there before.

The woman says, Only once or twice.

The man says, The food is good.

The woman says, The service, too.

The man says, How did we find that restaurant?

The woman says, My friend recommended it.

The man says, Your new friend.

The woman says, That's right, my new friend.

The man says, Your friend has good taste.

The woman says, For certain things, yes.

Clearly this means something. Clearly there is a double meaning here but the man doesn't care to get into it.

He says, I enjoyed the minestrone.

She says, I thought you would.

He says, I like to eat food that's been cooked by an old Italian widow.

She says, I think the chef is a Frenchman.

The chef she is referring to is an Algerian who speaks French. Everyone thinks he is French, but he's not. The chef has done nothing to set the record straight regarding his heritage.

He says, What about your friend?

She says, My friend is not an old Italian widow, either.

He says, Give her time.

She says, My friend doesn't need time.

He says, What does she need?

She says, Don't.

He says, Perhaps she would like to join us next time?

The woman looks at the man.

She says, I don't think so. She doesn't like Italian food.

He says, I thought she recommended it.

She says, She did.

He says, I understand.

She says, You understand nothing.

He says, You are probably right. I have never been good at understanding. All my life I've wanted to understand things. Something. Anything. I don't know.

She says, What don't you know?

He says, The simplest things—how a....

The man is trying to think of something to say.

He says, I can't even think of something simple. He says, It's always been a mystery.

This Algerian chef might be Italian.

He is swarthy.

He speaks French, but no one knows if he speaks Italian.

The man doesn't know this about the chef. This is one example of what the man doesn't know about the world.

The man doesn't understand so much about the world it is difficult to keep up with all he doesn't understand.

The man doesn't understand women, men, children, animals. He doesn't understand how anyone could be a vegetarian or a vegan. He doesn't understand how anyone can hold a nine-to-five job for more than six months at a time, how anyone can choose a career in politics, in business, in finance, in education, in farming, in industry of any kind.

He doesn't understand anything technical, anything having to do with math or geometry or electronics. He doesn't understand simple directions, be they directions on how to assemble a piece of furniture, say a television stand, or directions to an address.

He doesn't understand how the local baseball team cannot recognize that the first basemen has no future in major league baseball. He doesn't understand how the local football team continues to play the same quarterback.

He doesn't understand why hockey isn't more popular.

He doesn't understand the appeal of soccer or racing of any kind. Not car racing, horse racing, dog racing, or people racing on the street or on a track. He doesn't understand long-distance racing especially, doesn't understand how anyone can ever go jogging.

This is only a partial list of what the man doesn't understand.

What the man doesn't know would fill an even longer list.

She says, I think I'm hungry.

It seems as if she's changing the subject. This is something she feels comfortable doing. She always has another subject at the ready for such occasions.

It's not clear if she's actually hungry, though. She has eaten at least one pastry since coming downstairs, since sitting down at the breakfast table.

The woman has a peculiar metabolism.

She is often hungry. She is an advocate of eating several small meals throughout the day rather than eating the traditional breakfast, lunch, and dinner. She is also an advocate of snacking in between these several meals. She calls it grazing.

One would think the woman would be portly, if not rotund, but she is not.

She is stout, solid, average.

She has dimensions, measurements.

She is a woman, like millions of others.

He says, Well. If I did understand and your friend was an old Italian widow, I would like to eat her food. That's what I'm saying here.
She says, I don't believe that's what you're saying.
He says, I speak plain and to the purpose. I'm not clever enough for double meanings.
She says, Well, I will tell her that the next time we speak.

He says, Will you ask if she is naked?
She says, If I remember.
He says, I don't think you will.
She says, Perhaps not.
He says, Where does your friend live now?
She says, Why is this important?
He says, I didn't say it was important.

The woman's friend is a nudist. Obviously the man is fascinated by this.

If he's not exactly fascinated by the woman's nudism, then he sees it as an opportunity to needle his wife. His wife has strange, freewheeling, eccentric friends. Friends who go on about saving the whales and the rainforests and the seals, any and all endangered species, and the drinking water.

The man knows that the friend has recently moved. He remembers his wife telling him about this move over dinner one night.

Otherwise, he overheard this one Sunday morning when his wife was on the telephone.

Sometimes he eavesdrops on her Sunday morning conversations with this friend.

There is probably nothing to read into this behavior beyond curiosity.

They named the poodle Jasper, after the man's father. Jasper is his father's middle name. Apparently, the man was almost named Jasper himself but his parents changed their minds when filling out the birth certificate.

The man and woman didn't think of this as an homage, but that's how his father took it.

They saw it more as a joke.

The man found the early rearing of the poodle difficult, from simple behavior modification to housebreaking.

The dog spent a lot of time and slept in what is called a crate but is effectively a cage. The dog looked like a prisoner inside of the crate and was always reluctant to go back inside after being allowed to roam free.

On occasion the man and woman had to lure the dog back into the crate with food.

They fed the dog a raw diet, which was recommended by their holistic veterinarian.

This raw diet consisted of organic chicken backs and beef tripe. The man would go to the natural food store once a week to stock up on chicken backs and beef tripe.

The man couldn't understand how anyone could eat this food, including dogs.

The man couldn't understand why they couldn't feed their dog what everyone else in the world feeds their dog.

The man has always been delicate and doesn't like to see the dog eat his meals, particularly the beef tripe. He does listen to the bones breaking when the dog devours the chicken backs. There is something about this he enjoys, the primal carnality of it. But he never watches the dog eat the beef tripe. The first and only time he watched, he saw the dog gnawing on the beef tripe in a futile attempt of slicing it, which seems impossible with beef tripe. At some point the dog choked down a large chunk of it and the man sat there, astonished. He was certain the dog would die on the spot and he'd be called upon to resurrect him.

It's probably no surprise that the man could never bring himself to clean up after the poodle's many accidents. He'd call out to his wife and say something like, There is a problem in the living room or The vestibule has been contaminated.

Eventually the poodle became housebroken. It took five weeks or years.

She says, I've thought about what it would be like if she lived closer. If she were more accessible. I can't say I'd be comfortable.
He says, Why is that?

She makes a face that indicates she doesn't know.

He says, I understand.
She says, I am supposed to see her tomorrow for lunch.
He says, Ask if she knows any old Italian widows. Any woman whose husband died years ago from cancer or liver disease.
She says, There is something wrong here.
He says, I like to sit at a table reading a newspaper while the widow staggers around the kitchen. I like to watch her retrieve oregano from the spice rack and mozzarella from the icebox. That's what she calls it, the icebox. One of the six best words of the English language.
She says, It's a good one, yes.
He says, A woman that can bury her husband in the morning and fry eggplant for supper that evening is from another time and place. I like to watch her talk to herself as she browns the garlic in olive oil and washes the basil leaves. She's wearing this blue house-

coat, this frayed and tattered housecoat, and her pockets are stuffed full of novenas and soiled tissues, and this stinking housecoat doesn't fully cover the network of varicose veins up and down her old spider legs, legs that can barely keep her upright, legs that no one in the world wants to catch sight of, but you can bet your ass the housecoat matches the blue slippers, that's her outfit, she wears it every day, and these slippers, Jesus, these grimy slippers that fail to cover bony toes, toes that turn in absurd impossible directions, toes that arthritis or some other disease has made a shambles of. Jesus Christ, those goddamned toes. There's no way you can eat rigatoni after seeing something like that. But goddammit, you do it anyway. You eat the rigatoni.

She says, This widow—who is she?

He says, I don't know.

He says, I'm not sure. I think she was the friend of a friend's mother growing up. She cooked for me every weekend. I loved her.

This woman wasn't the friend of a friend's mother, but rather the friend's mother herself. She wasn't an old woman, either, but she seemed like it to the man, with the understanding that the man was a boy then.

This woman was indeed a widow, but her husband died in a car accident and not from cancer or liver disease. The man was in perfect health at the time of his death except for the occasional bout with diverticulitis.

The boy never sat at a table reading a newspaper while this woman staggered around the kitchen retrieving oregano and mozzarella from the icebox. This woman never staggered at all; in fact, she was graceful, almost like a dancer. As a younger woman, she studied ballet, and years later could still pirouette and plié.

This woman never referred to the appliance as an icebox, but rather a refrigerator. It's possible she called it a Frigidaire.

This woman did wear a blue housecoat, but her pockets were never stuffed with novenas and soiled tissues. She was agnostic and carried handkerchiefs.

Her legs were smooth and unsullied and never featured a network of varicose veins, nor were her toes misshapen, despite her training as a ballerina.

The man is confusing this woman with a great-aunt, who is almost exactly as he describes.

She says, You will eat anything—it's all par for the course, as per usual.

He says, Yes, indeed.

She says, Anything hot, anything partially cooked. Something that was once alive, breathing. You are usual again. You are being usual.

He says, Usual. Usual is funny to me. U JEW AL. It sounds ridiculous, phonetically, the phonetics of it. All words do in the end, sound ridiculous. Language is ridiculous, arbitrary and ridiculous. We are talking noises here. How do we distinguish these noises, this language of ours, from gibberish? What's the difference? You listen to other languages, for example. You listen to German, Chinese, Swahili, Greek. Goddammit if that doesn't sound like gibberish to me. I look at those people and I wonder how the hell do they know what they're saying to each other. Can you distinguish one word from the next in those languages? Can you distinguish one word from a grunt or a groan?

She says, I can't, no.

He says, That's what I mean.

She says, They understand each other. If you spoke German or Chinese or Swahili, you would understand, too.

He says, I doubt it.

She says, I doubt it, too, now that I think of it.

He says, English is the only language I'm capable of speaking.

She says, If that.

The man will not eat anything, as there are certain foods he has no interest in. Beef tripe, first and foremost. Of course, he enjoys meat—beef, fowl, pork. He is a man, American. He does eat vegetables, particularly as he's reached middle age. He doesn't want to contract colorectal cancer or any related catastrophe. He always indulges in grains, breads, cereals, pastas, as he believes them to be a staple.

The man does most of the cooking.

The woman is content with grazing, and as such has never prepared the kinds of meals the man enjoys.

She will contribute a salad and her version of coleslaw.

Before they were married, she would make her version of coleslaw on a Monday and have it for the rest of the week.

Her coleslaw includes both red and green cabbage, carrot, a light dressing consisting of olive oil and honey, salt and pepper. There is no mayonnaise in her coleslaw.

The man took Spanish in both junior high school and high school, but he couldn't retain much of it. Subsequently, he received poor grades.

He received poor grades throughout his scholastic career. He graduated 78th in a class of 118.

In Spanish he knows how to say hello, how are you, and perhaps a few other phrases.

He also knows how to say hello, how are you in Polish, though he never studied Polish in high school. Polish wasn't a part of the curriculum. He assumes Polish isn't part of the curriculum anywhere in America.

He learned how to say hello, how are you in Polish from the woman that went away.

This is all she taught him how to say.

The woman was leaving in the morning and she wanted to teach him how to say something in Polish before she left. For some reason she thought this was important.

They went back to her apartment after the going away party and this is where she conducted the lesson. The man had a hard time pronouncing the *how are you* part of the phrase, but soon mastered it. The woman told him his accent was funny.

The man was pleased to learn how to say something in Polish and he wondered why she never taught him this before. He wanted to ask her this question, but decided against it.

He was hoping they'd have intercourse one last time and he thought questions and answers wasn't any kind of foreplay.

There were some initial attempts at intercourse, pushing and pulling, arms and legs, awkwardness and frustration. Finally they gave up when she said she couldn't, when she said stop it.

She was going overseas, back to where she'd come from, where she was raised. It's not clear if she was raised in Poland, though. She had at times indicated she was Romanian and at other times had said something about Slovakia.

She would probably return in a year or two, hoping to maybe pick her life back up where she was leaving it off, leaving it behind. This is what she told everyone she knew, including the man and including her husband back home.

The man knew about the husband back home.

She told him theirs was an open marriage, that it'd always been complicated, that she didn't see it lasting forever but he was her husband and she needed to try.

She told him that he shouldn't wait for her, but left open whatever might be possible.

She said all of it was regrettable and unfair.

She did imagine reuniting with the man upon her return and him greeting her in Polish.

This never happened.

The man is impressed by anyone who is bilingual or multilingual. He cannot fathom how anyone can be proficient at more than one language.

The man, too, has never traveled abroad, and his inability to speak another language is part of the reason. He hasn't told anyone this, including his wife.

The woman has suggested they travel to Europe any number of times over the years but the man has always maintained that they can't afford it. He is leery of overextending themselves. He's said traveling for its own sake is frivolous.

But he says they'll do it someday.

He says, What came first?
She says, What first?
He says, Language. We're talking about language now.
She says, I thought we were talking about my friend.
He says, We're talking about her, too.
She says, I forgot you are versatile.
He says, So, what came first?
She says, It depends.
He says, On one hand we have sounds, we have physiology. The tongue, lungs, larynx, and whatever else is involved in making sounds.
She says, Language is what gets us in trouble.
He says, Did one person come up with the word for spear, for meat, for fire? Did the clan monkey-see-monkey-do after this one person?
She says, Language and liquor.
He says, Then we have the written symbols. Drawings—such and such indicates a letter, a string of letters indicates a word, and so on.
She says, Indeed.
He says, I know. There are no answers.
She says, Only the conversation.
He says, The repartee.
She says, The back and forth.

It wasn't long after the dog became housebroken that he developed health problems.

There was always something wrong with his eyes and ears. Pus would ooze out of these areas and the woman would do her best to keep these areas free and clear and clean.

The holistic veterinarian prescribed drops for both the eyes and ears. The man would hold the dog in place while the woman applied the drops.

The dog would periodically go off his feed, develop other infections, and sustain injuries that resulted in limping, that resulted in the man carrying him up and down the stairs.

During this time, the man thought of the dog as a lemon. He mentioned this to his friend.

He said he'd be stuck with the lemon for fifteen years.

The friend is right now at home, in his basement, hiding from his own wife, Janice.

He is also looking for a bottle of whiskey to bring over later. He keeps bottles of whiskey in the basement so his wife won't find them.

He is chewing on a toothpick and fumbling with a tarp, as he cannot recall where he's hidden any of the bottles.

The friend doesn't have a dog, as his wife, Janice, doesn't like animals.

The friend's wife, Janice, is a practicing vegetarian and occasionally dabbles in veganism.

The irony of this mystifies everyone.

Eventually, though, the man grew to feel genuine affection for the poodle.

The dog was sleeping in the crate, which was now placed in their bedroom upstairs.

They initially had the crate downstairs but moved it upstairs after the dog whimpered ceaselessly several nights in a row. The man said he couldn't take this anymore and the woman said I know.

It was in the middle of the night when the dog started vomiting. The man had never heard a dog vomit before and the noise startled him. They rushed over to the dog, who seemed perfectly at ease.

This was some kind of turning point for the man.

The woman said, See, you love him, too.

The man didn't have to resurrect the dog, but he was prepared to do so.

He says, About your friend. Was she naked?
She says, I don't know, why don't you call her back and ask?
He says, She doesn't like me.
She says, She likes you.
He says, Has she indicated such?
She says, Not to me, she hasn't.
He says, Then how do you know?
She says, I don't. It's only a guess.
He says, It's all guesswork, our entire lives.

There is quiet. They are reading. It seems as if they are finished with the pastries, but probably not with the conversation.

He says, How do you know her again?
She says, I've always known her.
He says, I thought she was a new friend.
She says, She is, yes, but I've always known her.
He says, Yes, but how?
She says, I don't remember.
He says, How can you not remember?
She says, I don't know.
He says, Well, then.

Around the same time the dog developed health problems, the man developed problems of his own.

These problems included overactive bladder or enlarged prostate, carpal-tunnel syndrome, tinnitus, some sort of kidney infection, vertigo, and anxiety.

The man also developed a sleep disorder.

He'd wake with a start, believing he was dead. He'd fly out of the bed and run over to the window for air, his heart beating audibly. Thirty or so seconds later, he'd come to and calm down, realizing he wasn't dead, that everything was more or less fine.

Otherwise, he'd jerk upright and put his hands on the woman.

The first time he did this the woman didn't know what to think.

Eventually she grew accustomed to this disorder, as she had with his other disorders.

She'd urge the man to see a sleep doctor but he'd say something about overextending themselves.

During this time the woman's own health problems continued. She still had asthma, still wheezed through the night.

She still had TMJ and fibromyalgia, which the husband couldn't believe was an actual condition.

Also, she contracted Lyme disease one weekend while visiting the cabin upstate.

Whatever the minor procedure corrected seemed more or less fine.

Fibromyalgia is a chronic condition characterized by pain in the muscles, ligaments, and tendons; fatigue; and multiple tender points on the body. While no one knows what causes fibromyalgia, it is believed to involve psychological, genetic, neurobiological, and environmental factors. There is evidence that people with the condition may be more sensitive to pain because something is wrong with the body's usual pain perception processes. More women than men have fibromyalgia, which doesn't surprise the man at all. Fibromyalgia tends to come and go throughout life, which also doesn't surprise the man. The whole thing seems arbitrary and capricious.

The condition or syndrome tends to coexist with sleep disorders, anxiety, depression, and irritable bowel syndrome.

The woman, indeed, has all of these.

The woman can spend days on end in bed, only leaving to visit the bathroom. During these times, she asks her husband to sleep in the guest room.

The guest room has a futon that is not at all comfortable. After two or three days, the man will go into the master bedroom and say, I can't take the futon anymore. The woman will say, I know.

The woman takes various muscle relaxants and tranquilizers during these episodes of prostration.

The man wasn't aware of these episodes of prostration until well into the courtship.

That's what he calls the episodes—prostrations. He'll tell his friend that his wife is prostrate in bed again. He'll talk about the futon, how he can't take it, specifically the bar running down the center, how he can feel it through the thin mattress.

He decided to ignore these prostrations, hoping that maybe one day she'd get better.

Out of everything wrong with her, this is perhaps most troubling.

The man will spend entire days researching these conditions on the Internet. He's not sure he believes anything he reads, and at the same time he is convinced that something is very wrong.

She did say early on, one night over dinner, that there were some things she hadn't told him yet. She said they had to do with certain medical issues, family histories, genetics. She told him she'd understand whatever decision he might make at any time.

This was the same night she told him she might not be able to get pregnant. Not only did she suspect an inability to conceive, but she also doubted she could carry a child and then deliver it successfully.

The man asked if a doctor had told her this and she said no. She said she had a feeling.

The man told her not to fret over this. He said there were other options.

He wasn't sure what he meant by this and was grateful she didn't ask or agree.

They both agree how they are cared for medically is guesswork. They each have visited traditional doctors, homeopathic doctors, alternative therapists, talk therapists, acupuncturists. They have taken herbs and supplements. They have changed their diets.

They haven't tried exercise, as neither is physically capable of exercise anymore.

Years ago the man was a gifted athlete. But he has been inert for twenty years.

Every part of the woman's body hurts. Her whole body is killing her.

Whenever the man exerts himself, his legs will burn. Even during a leisurely walk in the park.

No one knows exactly what is wrong with them or how to address it.

They are typical. They are Americans.

She says, Are you hungry?
He says, Do you think it strange that I've not seen her for so long now?
She says, No. Do you think it strange we've not seen your father for so long now?
He says, Then what do you base your guess on?
She says, What guess is this again?
He says, Your friend.
She says, Yes, I remember. Most people like you. Most people seem to enjoy your company. Surely you've noticed this.

He says, Maybe I have and maybe I haven't. What I don't know is...

She says, There are people who seem to enjoy having you in their company. They seem to enjoy having you in close proximity. They enjoy drinking with you, talking with you, dancing with you, engaging in all kinds of exotic behaviors.

He says, I'm not sure that's true.

She says, Well, we both know differently.

The man and woman have struggled financially.

The woman is a licensed acupuncturist and was hoping her private practice would take off in this community.

The people in this community seem typical and unwell. They seem as if they would patronize a licensed acupuncturist just as they do the local yoga studio.

So far this has not been the case.

Two of the few clients she's been able to procure are the neighbors who were out walking the dog earlier.

She dragooned them into booking an appointment while they were helping clean a mom-and-pop delicatessen that had been flooded during the most recent hurricane.

One came in for high blood pressure, the other general maintenance.

Right now, the neighbors are probably napping. The dog is probably asleep, too.

The woman sees maybe two or three patients a week.

Sometimes she calls them patients, other times clients.

The rest of the time she's had to find work in various nursing homes as an occupational therapist.

Occupational therapy is the use of treatments to develop, recover, or maintain the daily living and work skills of patients with a physical, mental, or developmental condition. It focuses on adapting the environment, modifying the task, teaching the skill, and educating the client/family in order to increase participation in and performance of daily activities, particularly those that are meaningful to the client.

Most of her patients suffer from dementia or have had strokes or some other kind of debilitating injury.

She teaches them to make coffee, balance a checkbook.

Their own checkbook is often out of balance.

They sometimes do the math together at the kitchen table. This is usually after dinner and never on Sundays.

One says something like, I'm not sure we can make this work. The math doesn't add up.

The other agrees.

They are referencing the mortgage, the second mortgage, the home equity loan, the bills, their lives.

Part of the problem has been the upstairs bathroom, which needed to be gutted and then reassembled a couple of years ago. This process involved a contractor, painters, plumbers.

The man was charged with taping off the doorways so that the dust didn't spread all over the house and inflame the woman's asthma.

He says, People sometimes....
She says, Of course, people.
He says, Do you want breakfast?
She says, I don't think so.
He says, Are you not hungry?
She says, I don't think I am, no.

Sometimes the pastries are not enough. Sometimes one or the other will make bacon and eggs. They will make toast, too, to go along with the bacon and eggs. She prefers either whole wheat or multigrain; he enjoys rye, be it seedless or no.

He is supposed to avoid seeds and nuts due to his diverticulitis.

Most of the doctors and other medical practitioners have advised him to avoid seeds and nuts. However, the latest research on diverticulitis has found no linkage between the aggravation of diverticulitis with the consumption of seeds and nuts. In fact, it now appears that a higher intake of seeds and nuts can help to avoid diverticulitis in adult males.

He says, My father doesn't get around like he used to.
She says, This means what?
He says, Why we haven't seen him.
She says, I'm sure that's part of it.
He says, Sometimes the answer is clear.
She says, Except when it isn't.

They look at each other again, past and through.

One sips coffee, the other doesn't. Neither bites into a pastry.

Outside on the street, there is a sedan parked directly across from their front gate, which is directly across from the front door.

The car is colored like the pages of an old book, somewhere between yellow and air. There is probably a word for this shade, but the man and woman don't know anything about cars. There are rust spots scattered about the hood, roof, and doors, what might be dubbed the body of the car. One assumes the previous owner had the car painted by professionals, though not the same outfit that painted the house. It is doubtful a car would be made available to the public in this color by the manufacturer.

There are a number of dents, as well. The most conspicuous is located on the driver's side door. Whatever accident caused the damage had to have been serious. Perhaps there were injuries, fatalities.

The car has been out there for a week.

Last night the man said something about the car.

He said, Do you know whose car is parked outside?
She said, No.

Between the car and house, on either side of the gate, are hedges.

The outer rim of the property is lined with hedges.

This was a selling point for the woman, the hedges. She liked how they looked and that they afforded a certain privacy.

The man wondered who would maintain the hedges and the rest of the property, which included a rather large and uneven lawn.

Turns out the man was charged with maintaining the lawn and grounds for the first few months. He mowed once a week, which was trying and difficult, but trimmed the hedges, which took hours, only once. Mowing was a slow walk in the park compared to trimming the hedges.

Trimming the hedges involved ladders and extension cords and chargers and gloves and reaching and leaning and was a total misadventure.

The hedges were misshapen like an old widow's arthritic toes.

The woman took one look at the hedges and said A child could do better.

The man feigned an allergy attack the next time he mowed the lawn and attempted to do the hedges.

He sneezed and rubbed and scratched and gasped and wheezed and finally said I can't take this anymore and the woman said, I know.

They hired landscapers the next day even though they couldn't afford landscapers then and still can't.

The man wonders who the car belongs to, if anyone. It looks abandoned. It looks like it was involved in something heinous and illegal.

Their own cars are parked in the driveway of their freestanding garage.

This is the driveway the slugs have maneuvered through on their way to other pastures, though none are green on account of the sunburnt lawn.

The man and woman have a freestanding garage, which is often a feature of a Cape Cod.

The garage is located behind the house and actually sits on another street. Meaning their mailing address is on one street but the garage is on another.

They walk in and out of the house through the back door, which opens into a mud room.

He says, And the movie last night. I was also thinking about the movie.
She says, Did you like it?
He says, It was fine. It could've been better. I liked it well enough. What about you?
She says, It was something to do.
He says, So, you didn't like it?
She says, No.
He says, What was wrong with it, exactly?
She says, Exactly.
He says, I know what you mean. It was exactly familiar.
She says, The same thing all over again.

The man wants to talk about familiarity, about sameness and monotony, about predictability, about standardization and tedium, about uniformity. He wants to know why this is the norm, why everyone settles for this. He thinks everything is a repeat, a replication, some kind of formulaic simulacrum.

It's the everydayness of life that kills a man in the end.

He wonders if there are no alternatives, if the very nature of our humanity calls for these things, demands them.

He decides to speak up. There is time for him to speak his mind, as it is Sunday morning.

He says, It is dense, the way things go unattended. It's how it is every day here now, everyone uncertain, everyone feeling around in the dark for what might be right in front of them, unsure of their footing, hands extended, like a zombie in the old zombie movies or a mummy in the old mummy movies.

She says, There were no zombies or mummies in the movie last night.

He says, They couldn't have hurt, that much is certain.

The man looks at the woman but the woman is tracking a caterpillar climbing up the windowsill.

He says, There are too many people here, everywhere you go people, people with other people, people with older people, people making newer people, be it the bus depot or the public parkways or the city streets or even in your own kitchen, fighting your way through the zombies and mummies to boil a pot of water, maybe dropping some converted rice in there so you can have something to eat, so you can stay alive another day, but none stand a post anymore and check passes, check identifications and credentials, ask questions, conduct surveys, these zombies and mummies today go through the very slow motions and this is a problem because I'm talking about who is left to keep on top of things, how all of us should get up in the morning and go to work, how it is we should behave, who it is we should talk to and how it is we should talk.

There is no telling how the caterpillar got into the house. The woman suspects she accidentally brought it in when she was gardening yesterday.

The woman maintains a small vegetable garden in the backyard. She grows tomatoes and basil.

She says, When you're right...
He says, Sing it, sister.
She says, What is converted rice?

He says, I don't know.

She says, That's what you said, right?

He says, I do believe, yes.

She says, But you don't know what it is.

He says, I don't know quite a lot of what I say.

She says, There's no point arguing.

He says, I don't know what converted rice is but I like the sound of it. I like to think the rice used to be one religion but found another, it doesn't matter which or what, like it used to be a zombie but became a mummy after reading through a pamphlet, after listening to a sermon or two, after seeing the light, so now it is part of the flock, a member of the congregation, can go out into the overpopulated world and evangelize, see how many it can bring into the fold, see how many it can birth and baptize, so that everyone is crowded together everywhere, at bus stops and parkways and kitchens, everyone insisting upon staying alive another day, insisting upon procreation, upon locomotion, moving around the inundated world, hands extended in the dark and right in front of them, unsure of their footing, uncertain and unattended.

The caterpillar has attained the uppermost part of the windowsill. The molding is next.

She says, No one makes movies about bathrooms, about cleaning bathrooms.

He says, Maybe the French.

She says, Someone should make a movie about cleaning the bathroom for two hours because her father-in-law is in town visiting.

He says, Maybe the Italians.

She says, The trouble is, no one ever has a movie star scrubbing the sink, the mirror above the sink, the bathtub. They might have her in there for a minute or two, maybe she's smoking a cigarette, has her hair under a bandana, is wearing blue rubber gloves. She's in there cleaning and her husband is out with his best friend and his darling new wife, so she's cleaning the bathroom and drinking gin and listening to the stereo loud.

He says, All the filthy Europeans.

She says, But then as she is cleaning the phone rings and it will be the husband who is out with his best friend and his darling new wife, or it will be the best friend's darling new wife who is drunk and nearly incoherent, and they are all of them up to no good, and then on the phone they all talk gibberish to each other and maybe it sounds like Greek or Swahili but it doesn't matter because just then the father-in-law who is in town visiting will ring the doorbell and the father-in-law will approach the daughter-in-law and the daughter-in-law will tell him what she thinks is really happening and she will feel ridiculous because she knows the father-in law's story, she's seen how he operates, and he will comfort her and say there there, there there, and she will feel ridiculous and the next morning all of them will go together out for a pancake breakfast because you can't have the movie star in there cleaning the bathroom for more than two minutes. You can't have her hair under a bandana, drinking gin and talking to her father-in-law for too long. People won't stand for it and the movie star won't stand for it either.

He says, So what happens at the pancake breakfast?

She says, Nothing happens at the pancake breakfast. They all sleep through the alarm.

He says, That's too bad.

The caterpillar is out of sight. There is no telling where it has gone or what will become of it.

She says, But there should be a movie where the movie star is in the bathroom cleaning for the whole movie. She should drink a quart of gin and smoke four packs of cigarettes and keep all of her hair up under that bandana and listen to every album in her collection loud.

Do you understand what I'm telling you? Sometimes it takes that long to clean a bathroom. Sometimes the bathroom needs that kind of cleaning.

He says, It sounds like pornography.

She says, Everything sounds like pornography to you.

He says, There is definitely a double meaning in this. Now I have to figure out what it is.

The man doesn't want to figure out any double meanings now. He is tired and wants to go back to bed.

Also, he is comfortable with ignorance when it comes to certain matters.

The man is often tired, though he generally sleeps well, except when he has a night terror. The most recent one had him knocking over a nightstand and causing a brief ruckus.

His wife chided him after he calmed down. She said, Seriously, man.

The man glances at the sports section. The story he's most interested in concerns the recent struggles of the first baseman referred to earlier. This is quite possibly the worst baseball player the man has ever seen.

This first baseman is a power hitter, can hit the ball a long way when he makes contact, which he rarely does because he is quite possibly the worst hitter the man has ever seen. This first baseman's swing is long and full of holes. This first baseman cannot catch up to a fastball and is hopeless on anything off-speed. Anyone can get him out at any time and everyone does. It's extraordinary to the man how the general manager cannot recognize that this first baseman has no future playing major league baseball.

She says, Do you want more coffee?
He says, Yes, please.

The woman rises and walks across the kitchen to the countertop, where she picks up the coffee pot and fills her mug. She then brings the pot over to the kitchen table, where she refills her husband's mug. She sets the pot down on the sports section and retakes her seat.

He says, I wasn't reading that. She says, I'm sorry.
He says, Never mind.
She says, I'll try.
He says, That would be a good movie.
She says, I don't think so.
He says, I had an idea once, for a movie.
She says, What idea?
He says, I can't remember, but it was a good one.
She says, That's too bad.
He says, Now it's tree-fuckers and rancid seagulls for breakfast.
She says, I don't know what you're talking about.
He says, Neither do I.

What the man can't remember, his idea for a movie, isn't so much an idea for a movie, but rather a character in a movie, the star of it, and his foil, who serves as the narrator.

He thinks of himself as the foil and the star is someone called Alex the Unfortunate.

The movie starts with a narrated monologue while a sequence of shots depicts the foil in action, walking a series of barren streets at night, wandering into an empty barroom, sipping on a bourbon. The foil is shot from the back so we cannot see his face. He has on a brown leather jacket and walks with a slight limp.

The foil says, Alex the Unfortunate was the one born that way, unfortunate, but I wasn't. I was born beautiful, without blemish, with people wanting to take my picture, touch my skin and hold me close. Alex the Unfortunate was born unsightly, pockmarked and discolored, but I'm not Alex. I'm someone else. Maybe I look a little like Alex the Unfortunate, around the eyes, perhaps in pigmentation, but that's all. Alex the Unfortunate was born asthmatic, struggling for breath, wheezing. I was born healthy, like a horse, stout and hale and upright. They say I was born standing up and talking back and I believe them. Alex the Unfortunate was born meek, cowering in a corner, alone in the middle of a room, in the middle of the night, in the middle of nowhere, pacing back and forth, naked and confused. This isn't what happened to me. I was born like most people, in a hospital, surrounded by loved ones, knowing what was what and who was who. It wasn't until much later that Alex the Unfortunate was born catching cold, catching hell, catching as catch can, limp and weak, suffering and lame. For me it was easy, but it wasn't for Alex, not at all. We look nothing alike, except maybe for our faces, the general shape of them, like an almond, and the hair, some of it gray, but not all of it. But otherwise we are two separate people and have nothing to do with each other. Alex the Unfortunate was born as a hypothetical, an idea, a vague notion, a best guess, whereas I'm real, I'm tangible. I can bleed and spit and run and jump and hide and seek. Whenever I am called Alex, I don't chastise people. I don't humor them, either, but I do accept apologies. I am always gracious, but the same can't be said for Alex. The truth is it doesn't bother me, none of it, not to any great extent. Whenever I see Alex, I am always cordial. I always say Hello Alex and Goodbye Alex and It was good running into you. So what I'm saying is, don't ever call me Alex.

This monologue takes about thirty minutes of screen time.

All the while you see the foil in action or inaction.

Clearly the narrator is Alex the Unfortunate and it's a case of mistaken identity or denial.

The man hasn't thought of this in years.

He wrote this opening and the outline of a story and sent it off to a friend of a friend who was in the business.

For weeks he checked the mail every day hoping to hear back.

The man has always enjoyed an anti-hero and thinks of himself as one, though no one else thinks of him this way.

He says, These things don't amount to anything. The trees and cars. The seagulls. It's like zero plus zero times zero, divided by zero.
She says, Say that two times fast.
He says, I think I can say almost anything two times fast.
She says, Say that two times fast.

They go back to reading and read like this for five minutes or hours or years. Then the woman gets up and walks over to the kitchen counter, where she dons yellow rubber gloves and does the dishes.

The man rises and leaves the kitchen.

Perhaps he checks on the car parked directly in front of the house. It is still out there.

Perhaps he considers doing something drastic, like fleeing the country or helping with the dishes.

Otherwise, he goes upstairs and tries to nap.

END OF ACT I

ACT II

The setting is the same, the same kitchen as before. The same table and chairs and all the rest.

It is later the same Sunday, now midafternoon.

The man is back at the table.

Presumably he napped earlier, after he had pastry and read the newspaper with his wife.

The man isn't sure if he actually napped, though napping was his intention.

He did not sleep well last night. Nor has he slept well this whole week.

He thinks he only dozed for an hour or so.

He was listening to the baseball game on the radio and the last thing he remembers is the first baseman striking out with the bases loaded.

But then the next thing he remembers is the first baseman making an error the very next inning.

If he had fallen asleep, he didn't stay asleep for long.

Across from the man, sitting in the same seat the woman occupied earlier, is the man's friend.

On the table is a bottle of unopened whiskey and two small bowls.

Each man is drinking a beer.

It is not important what kind of beer, foreign or domestic, bottled or canned. For specificity's sake let's say it is a bottle of beer, ale from England. Specificity is sometimes a comfort or luxury, but is often unnecessary.

The pastries are no longer on the table. The pastry box is now in the refrigerator.

Perhaps tomorrow the man will take one out of the refrigerator and eat it.

One man says to another, we are speaking in hypotheticals now. We all know this can't happen in real life.

The man's friend is the one who says this, but it applies to both.

This is something the man could've just as easily said.

The friend is referring to his marriage, the one he's been in for less than a year.

Before that, he drifted in and out, found himself in a few situations, different places.

This friend is here only in relation to the man. He has no life of his own, not to speak of. Yes, he is married. Yes, he sleeps in a queen-sized bed next to his wife, Janice, and drinks orange juice every morning and chews on toothpicks throughout the day, but otherwise, he can't be bothered.

This is what the man thinks sometimes, but not all the time.

His friend does have a life of his own, of course.

The friend says, In real life, this is someone who needs help. This is someone we call 911 for.
The man says, I know.
The friend says, We call in the Marines, the Red Cross.
The man says, It's all too much.

The man's friend woke early this morning, made breakfast but didn't eat it. The man's friend has lost his appetite. He's not sure what's wrong with him. His wife, Janice, wants him to see a doctor. He told her he would if his appetite doesn't return in a week or two, if he starts losing weight.

This morning he looked out the window and considered a running jump.

Instead he watched the television news. Somewhere in Asia people were being wiped out by a sequence of natural disasters. On the home front, some locals had gotten into trouble with the police and now the whole town was up in arms.

His wife, Janice, was still sleeping.

His wife, Janice, enjoys sleeping and sleeps up to fourteen hours a night. She doesn't wake until after noon most days.

The friend is married to a woman named Janice, who folds everything. She folds towels and sheets and paper napkins, folds plastic bags, cardboard boxes, anything that can be folded.

The friend has height and weight and a steady income, though he no longer works. He lives a daily life. He drives a reliable car, one with four doors and two speakers. He uses his fingers to eat, shave, and write notes to his wife, Janice. The notes concern the locals or what he hears on the news. His wife, Janice, folds the notes up neatly, sometimes making paper airplanes out of them.

The friend says, Today I got nothing done. I had a list but I accomplished nothing. I planned this and wound up with that.

The man says, Some days are exactly this way.

The friend says, I woke up and put on the news. I like to know what's going on. There's nothing wrong with wanting to know what's going on.

The man says, People don't know what's going on.

When the man says people don't know what's going on he's including himself, as he likewise doesn't know what's going on. He used to keep up with current events but it was too much for him after a while. Now he'll scan the headlines on Sunday, but that's it. He only reads the sports section with any interest.

The friend says, After the news I was going to mow the lawn, but then the phone rang.

The man says, The lawn will keep till tomorrow.

The friend says, Almost everything will keep until tomorrow until it can't anymore. Take my car; it needs an inspection. Why they need to inspect it is something I don't know. It seems fine to me.

The man says, I'm sure the car is fine.

The friend says, They ticketed me last week at the train station, so now I'm supposed to get the inspection and then bring the empties to the beer distributor. There are too many bottles in the garage and I broke two this past week. This should be easy for a grown man.

The man says, Nothing's easy.

The friend says, I'm not sure anymore. I remember getting dressed, turning off the TV. Or maybe I didn't turn it off so much as I turned the channel. I think I found a ballgame. Goodbye inspection, goodbye bottles is the end result.

The man says, I wouldn't know about that.

The friend says, I need to call the credit card company, too. They made a mistake on the bill. I wouldn't know this myself. My wife, Janice, told me. She's the one who checks the bills. After she pays the bills she folds them up and puts them in a file cabinet. I should call her and apologize. I also need to make an appointment with the doctor, get a prescription refilled.

The man says, Modern medicine.

The friend says, Life ain't worth living, death ain't worth dying.

The man says, That's like poetry.

The friend says, I can't help it sometimes.

These two have known each other for years. They grew up together. Their parents knew each other, too, and were friends themselves, for a time.

The man's mother divorced the man's father and thus ended the friendship.

All of this took place two states away.

How they ended up in the same neighborhood is the man's friend coaxed the man and woman into moving here. He said it was a great place to live. He said he knew of a Cape Cod about to go on the market. He said the woman could easily start up a new practice here. He said the people were typical and unwell and needed acupuncture. He said her practice would thrive and they'd thank him one day.

The woman has been unable to establish a healthy practice. She has tried advertising in local weeklies, hanging flyers at the supermarket.

It's possible she resents the man and his friend for this.

The man and friend know nothing of this possible resentment.

It's likely the woman is equally unaware.

The friend says, People talk to me like it's fun and games.
The man says, It isn't either.
The friend says, This is what I'm saying.
The man says, You've said this for years.
The friend says, Whenever people talk I think of spillage.
The man says, Makes sense.
The friend says, People spilling all over each other constantly.

It's not clear what the friend is referring to here, but the man is happy to play along.

The friend says, This is what happens: I wake up, sometimes in the morning. There is nothing to do. It's like zero plus zero every day around here and it never changes. I don't know much about math but it's like the saying says, I'm almost sure.
The man says, I couldn't agree more or less.
The friend says, Still, I can't say I'm entirely sure about anything, except for how I wake up, sometimes in the morning, with nothing to do. I could make breakfast and then eat it, sure, but then what. I would only have to eat lunch a few hours later. Anyone can see what I mean, where I'm going.
The man says, I'm with you.
The friend says, This is important to me.
The man says, I thought you lost your appetite.

Due to Janice's sleeping habits, the man's own have altered. It is true he wakes up every day, sometimes in the morning. But it's just as likely for him to wake up after noon. It's also true he has nothing to do since the accident.

The man suffered an accident on the job six months ago and is on disability.

It's not important who or what caused the accident or what the job was or what exactly the nature of his injury was and whether or not the friend has embellished the effects of the accident to his own benefit or detriment, depending on how one looks at such things.

The friend belongs to a union.

The friend says, These days, when I am in the house, I look out of windows. I almost never do anything but look out of windows in the house anymore. I go from one window to the next, both upstairs and down, front and back. I spend an hour or so at each window. My wife, Janice, doesn't approve. She would rather I spend time on a different hobby or else stay at one window all day. She'd also like it if I left the house, participated in the outside world.

The man says, Why would she want you to stay at one window all day?

The friend says, She doesn't say.

The man says, Maybe she wants to know where you'll be at any given time. Maybe she wants to keep tabs.

The friend says, I don't think that's the case.

The man says, You don't get bored doing this?

The friend says, I am on the lookout.

The man says, What are you looking for?

The friend says, That doesn't matter to me.

The man says, You are out of the house today. Here you are, out of the house.

The friend says, Out of the house.

The two men extend their respective bottles and say, Out of the house, in unison.

The origins of trade unions can be traced back to eighteenth-century Britain, where the rapid expansion of industrial society then taking place drew women, children, rural workers, and immigrants into the workforce in large numbers and in new roles. This pool of unskilled and semi-skilled labor spontaneously organized in fits and starts throughout its beginnings, and would later be an important arena for the development of trade unions. Trade unions have sometimes been seen as successors to the guilds of medieval Europe, though the relationship between the two is disputed, as the masters of the guilds employed workers who were not allowed to organize.

There was a time when the man and friend lost track of each other. They didn't speak for four or five years. Neither can remember what had happened to provoke or warrant this.

The man says, What do you see out the window?

The friend says, Much as you'd expect. Passersby, bystanders, neighbors, acquaintances. The odd salesman, the odd bird, the odd lost dog. I look at the weather, I track the sun's progress across the sky. If it's raining I note how it's coming down, straight or sideways, in sheets or drops.

The man says, And you don't get bored by this?

The friend says, It's the world we live in.

The friend is correct that this is the world we live in. There are passersby and bystanders, neighbors and acquaintances. It's impossible to determine just how many passersby and bystanders there are at any particular time.

All of it depends upon who is doing what and where, if anyone is doing anything at all and if either are offended.

Certainly passersby have to pass by something.

Of course there must be at least one person at this fixed point to observe the passersby passing by.

A bystander is generally present at an event without participating in it.

The event can be anything, but is generally tragic.

Which isn't to say that all events are tragic, only that when the word *bystander* is invoked it generally means that someone is standing by a tragedy.

The word *innocent* almost always precedes the word *bystander*.

Passersby can pass by an event without participating in it, but as long as they don't break stride they remain a passerby.

If the passerby stops to look around, take in the scene, they become a bystander. Provided the event is still occurring.

It's unclear if one can be a bystander to an event that has concluded.

It's possible the man has been a bystander and a passerby and it's possible he's done more than stand or pass by during a particular event or occasion.

It's possible he has made things worse by standing by.

The man tries to remember something he has witnessed, something catastrophic.

The man cannot think of anything, which has always been a problem for him.

There are, of course, countless neighbors and acquaintances in the world. Some neighbors qualify as acquaintances.

There must be millions of birds and dogs in the world, too.

The friend lives several blocks away in a ranch house with his wife, Janice. This house is significantly larger than the Cape Cod and sits in a nicer part of town, even though it is only several blocks away.

The friend's house is less than a ten-minute walk from the man's house. Still, whenever one visits the other, they always drive.

The friend can blame the accident on having to drive and sometimes does, but he's always driven to the man's house.

The friend says, There's also the bus stop up the street. I can see it out of one window in one of the guest rooms if I wear my binoculars.
The man says, What do you see there?
The friend says, A curious lot.
The man says, I'm sure.
The friend says, They are all of them wrong about how they look and how they talk and what they think and how they stand and sit and wait for the bus. They are the wrong kind of people.
The man says, And you can tell that by just looking at them.
The friend says, It's not difficult.
The man says, Have you ever taken the bus?

The friend says, Why would I take the bus?

The man says, To see where it goes.

The friend says, I can go there in my car.

The man says, Where does the bus go?

The friend says, Hell if I know. Probably the city.

The man says, I'm not sure I've ever taken a bus in my life.

The friend says, You haven't missed anything.

Most people take the bus alone, either commuting to work or back home again. People don't often talk to strangers on buses. If one takes the bus with a companion they sometimes talk to each other. Their conversations are almost always tedious. They talk about their rotten children, how this one moved in with that one or how another was arrested on trumped-up burglary charges. Sometimes they discuss what they want for lunch and where they want it.

Nothing important is ever discussed on a bus.

Yesterday, though, on the bus the two friends are currently discussing, one young woman, probably no more than twenty-five, struck up a conversation with an elderly man. Both were dressed as if they were going to or coming from church.

The young woman relayed a story about her great-uncle and how he was a basket case after the stroke. She said it was terrible. She said they had to feed him porridge through a straw every day, that's all he could manage. She said he was down to ninety-five pounds, though he once was stout and imposing.

The elderly man said something like It sounds like he lived a full life, though he had no way of knowing this.

The young woman smiled and said he did.

Then the elderly man said something of his late wife and how she loved the beach, where they used to go every weekend. He said they'd take this very bus every Saturday morning. He said they'd spend hours there, the whole day if they could. He said that's how she died.

His wife loved to swim parallel to the shore. The elderly man never liked swimming himself, so he never joined his wife in the water. In the beginning, when they were first married, he'd watch her swim, as he wanted to keep an eye on her, make sure she was okay. But then he started to do other things. Mostly he read the newspaper, but he also ogled women. He tried not to do this when his wife was next to him, but sometimes he couldn't help it. She never admonished him for noticing other women, but she did ask him not to ogle.

The elderly man said he was eating a sandwich his wife had made, ham on rye, when he saw a team of lifeguards run into the water. At the time, he didn't even realize his wife had gone swimming. He'd lost track of her. Sometimes she'd go to the concession stand or the ladies' washroom or she'd shop the stores along the boardwalk.

But it was his wife they dragged to shore. He watched them try to revive her, those skinny teenage boys. He watched them beat her chest and blow into her mouth.

He said he hasn't visited the beach since. He said it doesn't matter, that wherever he goes his wife's ghost follows him.

The young lady said she was sorry this happened. She said, You poor thing.

She tried listening to the elderly man's story, but found that she started thinking about her uncle and hoped she wouldn't have to be the one that fed him today.

The man says, Yesterday I got nothing done, either. I also had a list. I went around the house with a pencil and pad.

The friend says, Is that right?

The man says, I wouldn't lie to you.

The friend says, What was on the list?

The man says, I can't remember. I accomplished nothing, is the bottom line. I got sidetracked.

The friend says, These things happen.

The man says, I had plans. I know that much. I set goals for the day.

The friend says, You're human.

The man says, I think I was supposed to call the landscaper.

The friend says, The yard looks good.

The man says, I think I was to call the landscaper but the phone rang and I forgot.

The friend says, That's what I said earlier.

The man says, Did you?

The friend says, Who called?

The man says, Wasn't it you?

The friend says, Did I call you yesterday?

The man says, I can't remember.

The friend says, Neither can I.

Neither called the other yesterday.

They did speak on the telephone two days ago, and this is when they made plans to get together this Sunday.

It's unclear if either spent any time on the telephone yesterday. They're not intentionally lying to each other, though.

It's unclear what prompted the men to lose track of each other. It's possible one felt betrayed or forsaken by the other. If such is the case, it probably involved a miscommunication, a letter lost in the mail, a message that was never returned.

It's just as likely that one or the other was busy for those four or five years and never thought of getting in touch.

The man says, The weather is a popular topic of conversation with people.

His friend looks at him, confused. He pulls a silver case out of his pocket, removes a toothpick and places it in his mouth.

The man says, The weather is a popular topic of conversation with people.

The friend says, Who was talking about the weather?

The man says, You were. You said you watch it from behind your windows.

The friend says, I said that an hour ago.

The man says, I was listening to you. The friend says, That's nice of you.

Each man takes a sip of beer. Both bottles are almost empty and soon they'll be ready for new ones.

Neither has made a move toward the bottle of unopened whiskey.

The man says, Nine times out of ten, when someone changes the subject, they change it to weather. Yesterday it was cold.

The friend says, Yesterday it rained.

The man says, Yesterday there was a great wind.

The friend says, I was inside all day yesterday.

The man says, It was cold, take my word for it. People took pleasure in telling each other this. Boy, it's cold out. I heard them. Otherwise, they took comfort in telling each other this. It is hard to tell sometimes with people.

The friend says, People always need confirmation, assurance. Comfort and cold.

The man says, I don't know what people take or what they need.

The friend says, The weather is always like the weather here and everyone knows it.

The man says, Still, people are like this with each other. They are like, is it cold outside or is it me? Is it cold enough for you, or is it me?

The friend says, You can separate people into two camps. The ones who ask questions that end with *or is it me* and those who don't.

The man says, I agree.

Sitting behind the young lady and elderly man on the bus, who by now had concluded their conversation, was a middle-aged man on his way to work. Every time this middle-aged man takes the bus there is a woman next to him or almost next to him; every time she is beautiful or close to beautiful, with hair and hands and havoc all cobbled together, with too much skin showing, exposed and beckoning. She'll have a skirt that stops mid- thigh and her legs are folded one over another or crossed at the ankle. And the middle-aged man is a victim or thinks of himself as a victim, an innocent, hollow and helpless, with other things to do, other responsibilities, on this very bus to work, to go earn a living, to provide for the family, for the wife and children safe at home in front of a fire, the picture of domesticity. And he'll get off at his stop and walk to work along streets littered with these selfsame beautiful women coming and going, off to work themselves, to shops and schools, to lunch dates with other women, maybe not quite as beautiful but maybe even more beautiful, where they discuss matters having both everything and nothing to do with anything.

The middle-aged man realizes that the key is resignation, surrender, acknowledging the comedy and futility. He knows he has to keep his head down on the bus and on the streets so he can go teach children basic civility, comportment, citizenship, whatever it is he is supposed to do for the children, reading and writing and the theory of everything, up there in front of them, on the board. Today children we discuss times tables and fractal geometry, tomorrow it's subjective predicates and semiotics and no this will not be on the midterm, and in next week's faculty meeting he'll have to address the absences and truancy, the poor attendance records, basic disinterest and fundamental indifference so that it reminds him of the one joke he has memorized, the one he tells students sometimes though most never get it, maybe some chuckle out of reflex, but it only serves to prove a greater point, the one that goes like this:

They asked the principal what was the main problem with the students here, ignorance or apathy, and she answered, I don't know and I don't care.

He wants to tell his colleagues this joke during the meeting but he decides against it. Instead he waits for the bell to go off so he can go back to the bus so he can go home and so he is on the bus keeping his head down, exhausted and drained, hopeless but for hope, no place for civility or comportment, no place for citizenry. And it's back home for a night of quiet contemplation or obliteration, for erasure, to pour one drink after another after another, for that hour-long shower before bed, for the sweet oblivion of a dreamless sleep, this he thinks as he exits at the rear of the bus, as he keeps his head down and walks the streets toward home, past the beautiful women doing likewise and as he approaches his building he reaches inside his pocket, happening upon the loose change and dollar bills mingling there, the key, such as it is, unlocking the door to home and hearth.

Neither principal has ever met this middle-aged man, nor will they.

These three will go their entire lives without ever meeting.

The shame of it is they'd all get along and become great friends. That is, if the man had the ability to make new friends, which he doesn't.

The friend says, That I like it cold and damp is of no importance to anyone. Of course, this only matters when I do make it out of the house.

The man says, When people say, Isn't it cold, I move my head up and down to indicate confirmation, assurance.

The friend says, When I am inside and looking out the window I sometimes listen to the forecasts. I think they are better at it than they used to be. They tell you what's going to happen next and why it's going to happen. There's always a front on the move, a system approaching.

The man says, It's always something.

The friend says, The local news channels all do the weather at the same time, so you have to be fast clicking back and forth. This I am good at. Even my wife, Janice, says I'm good at this. It is perhaps my greatest skill.

The man says, I thought you were looking out the window.

The friend says, I am.

The man says, How can you click back and forth while looking out the window?

The friend says, I'm versatile.

The man says, I am the same way.

The friend says, There's a television in every room and I always have it on. The first thing I do when I walk into a room is turn on the television. I always have the remote control on me so I can click back and forth.

The man says, Sounds confusing.

The friend says, It isn't for a grown man. They almost always agree, the forecasters.

The man says, In this way, they are like most people.

By now both men are drinking fresh beers and the whiskey bottle is open.

By now the man remembers this isn't a good idea. It's not a good idea for his friend to be over, drinking in the middle of the day, here at the kitchen table in his own house, the one he shares with his wife, who is out now doing something with other people but who will return soon enough.

It's not a good idea for them to have dinner together later.

He thinks about saying this out loud, but decides against it.

One is drinking his whiskey straight while the other has his mixed with soda.

It is not important which is which.

Both men will drink whiskey straight and mixed with soda depending on how they feel. There is no discernible pattern to their drinking habits in this regard.

The car is still outside. It hasn't moved.

What the man doesn't know is that the car has, in fact, been abandoned.

The man isn't sure how long the car has been out there. If he had to guess he'd guess less than a week. He'd be wrong, however, because the car has been there for almost two weeks now.

Whiskey is a distilled alcoholic beverage made from fermented grain mash. Various grains, which may be malted, are used for different varieties, including barley, corn, rye, and wheat. Whiskey is typically aged in wooden casks, generally made of charred white oak.

It is possible that distillation was practiced by the Babylonians in Mesopotamia in the second millennium BCE, with perfumes and aromatics being distilled, but this is subject to uncertain and disputed interpretation of evidence. The earliest certain chemical distillations were by Greeks in Alexandria in the first century CE, but these were not distillations of alcohol. Written records of distillation in Arabic begin in the ninth century, but again these were not distillations of alcohol. Distilling technology passed from the medieval Arabs to the medieval Latins, with the earliest records in Latin in the early twelfth century.

The earliest records of the distillation of alcohol are in Italy in the thirteenth century, where alcohol was distilled from wine. An early description of the technique was given by Ramon Llull. Its use spread through monasteries, largely for medicinal purposes, such as the treatment of colic and smallpox.

The man says, I watch a lot of television, too, and can give you a run for your money.

The friend says, Perhaps I can get a job in television.

The man says, Doing what?

The friend says, I'm not sure.

The man says, Perhaps you can be a critic.

The friend says, I don't want to criticize anyone whose job it is to make television. I wouldn't want to criticize producers or directors, writers or actors. They are all geniuses to me, even the ones who are bad.

The man says, You think that's true?

The friend says, I do, and, Who the hell am I to criticize those people?

The man says, You're right, who the hell are you?

The friend is a man who has height and weight like millions of others. He's older now than he was and he still likes to sing in the shower and he likes to shower often, which he'll do several times throughout the day. If he bothers to get dressed in the morning or early afternoon he'll put on trousers and a collared shirt and always a pair of brown leather shoes and sometimes that crusty bowler that he wears tilted down toward his left eye, askew. Women have always taken to him and still do, including his new wife, Janice.

He'd eat if he were ever hungry and he drinks when he's thirsty.

He still can feel thirst, and for this he is grateful.

The friend says, If during a particular revolution around the television dial, as I click from one to one hundred, a full revolution up and down the dial—if I can count twenty women on the television that I'd kill the mailman to have sex with, I tell myself to leave the house.

The man says, You can always count on wanting to have sex with the weather women.

Both men raise their glasses and say, To the weather women.

The man says, I was just talking about the mailman we had growing up. I think he meant the world to me.

The friend says, I doubt that.

The man says, You're probably right.

The friend says, Only sometimes.

The man says, You were saying.

The friend says, I was, I think, yes—there is no reason for this to be a reason to leave the house. But this is my reason. I leave it up to chance.

The man says, What are you talking about?

The friend says, Leaving the house because of what's on television.

The man says, That's right, the weather women.

The friend says, Once out of the house, I sometimes realize I've no business being outside like this.

The man says, Subject to people and bitter weather.

The friend says, The only thing that will keep me in the house is a submarine movie. Doesn't matter which one.

The man says, I'm with you there.

The friend says, Reverse the starboard engines, right full rudder, man overboard port side, all back full—I can't get enough.

The man says, It's like when I was a submariner.

The friend says, You were never on a submarine.

The man says, I thought about it. I can reverse the starboard engines and go all back full with the best of them.

The man never once considered joining the navy or any of the armed services.

His father, Jasper, had served in the Army and was stationed overseas for two years.

The man was never sure what his father did in the Army.

He thinks he was a private or a corporal and did whatever privates and corporals do. He never served in a war, but was on active duty when a president was assassinated.

The friend says, Aren't you afraid of the water? Didn't you almost drown once?

The man says, What's all back full mean?

The friend says, It's when they have to slam on the brakes.

The man says, Amazing what you can learn from watching television.

The friend says, How did you almost drown, again?

The man says, It was in the river. The current.

The friend says, That's right. What were you doing in the river?

The man says, Drowning.

The friend says, I mean were you on a boat, were you fishing, were you....

The man says, I was on a boat and coaxed into the water.

The friend says, Fuck you and the coaxing.

The man says, The lesson is, boats are dangerous, as are planes, cars, horses, any mode of transportation.

The friend says, Who coaxed you into the water?

The man says, An old girlfriend.

The friend says, Was she trying to drown you?

The man says, There was that side to her.

The friend says, It's exciting, when a woman tries to kill you.

The man says, They are always trying to kill you.

The concept of an underwater boat has roots deep in antiquity. Although there are images at the temples at Thebes of men using hollow sticks to breathe underwater while hunting, the first known military use occurred during the siege of Syracuse (about 413 BCE), where divers were used to clear obstructions according to the History of the Peloponnesian War. At the siege of Tyre in 332 BCE, Alexander the Great, according to Aristotle, again used divers. Later legends suggested that Alexander used a primitive submersible for reconnaissance missions. This seems to have been a form of diving bell, and was depicted in a sixteenth-century Islamic painting.

Although there were various plans for submersibles or submarines made during the Middle Ages, the Englishman William Bourne designed one of the first workable prototype submarines in 1578. His idea ultimately never got beyond the planning stage. The first submersible to be actually built in modern times was constructed in 1605 by Magnus Pegelius.

The first successful submarine was built in 1620 by Cornelis Jacobszoon Drebbel, a Dutchman in the service of James I of England. It may have been based on Bourne's design. It was propelled by oars and is thought to have incorporated floats with tubes to allow air down to the rowers. The precise nature of the submarine type is a matter of some controversy; some claim that it was merely a bell towed by a boat.

The men drink from the whiskey and chase it with beer.

Neither man notices a fly buzzing behind the curtain of the window they are sitting under.

The fly found its way into the house through a hole in the screen door yesterday afternoon.

The woman had left the door open in order to get some fresh air into the house.

She was outside in her garden, tending to the tomatoes while she was airing out the house.

The man was elsewhere, probably in the park trying to read a story about the local baseball team's struggling first baseman. He was distracted by a woman practicing yoga, though, and couldn't concentrate on the story.

The woman proved a fine distraction. Her body was lean and angular and looked beautiful and elegant in every pose.

The story the man couldn't concentrate on quoted any number of team officials supporting the struggling first baseman. They all said they were confident the struggling first baseman could straighten himself out at the big-league level. There was speculation they'd send him down to the minors, but they were trying to avoid this scenario if at all possible.

However, they did admit that at some point something had to change.

The first baseman isn't a good baseball player, is the problem. The organization was fooled into thinking he has potential because he has occasionally hit a series of meaningless home runs over the past two years.

The struggling first baseman has horrible mechanics at the plate. He holds his hands too low and has a significant hitch in his swing, which prevents him from catching up with high fastballs. And the struggling first baseman can't hit a curveball to save his mother's life, which was in peril last year due to a bout with breast cancer.

Today she is in remission.

In fact, she is back on the courts today, playing tennis again for the first time in a year.

Her oncologist, who also plays, gave her the green light to start exercising again.

She has good ground strokes and is solid at the net. But she has a herky-jerky motion while serving that is as awkward-looking as her son's flailing swings at curveballs in the dirt.

Every day the man hopes to hear that the team has sent the struggling first baseman to the minor leagues.

He's certain that once this happens the struggling first baseman won't be heard from again.

But of course, he hopes the struggling first baseman's mother stays in remission and leads a full and lengthy life, her only disappointment being her son's fleeting major league career.

The origins of the fifteen, thirty, and forty scores in tennis are believed to be medieval French. The earliest reference is in a ballad by Charles D'Orleans in 1435, which refers to quarante cinque, and in 1522 there is a sentence in Latin, "We are winning thirty, we are winning forty-five." However, the origins of this convention remain obscure. It is possible that clock faces were used on court, with a quarter move of the hand to indicate a score of fifteen, thirty, and forty-five. When the hand moved to sixty, the game was over. However, in order to ensure that the game could not be won by a one-point difference in players' scores, the idea of "deuce" was introduced. To make the score stay within the sixty ticks on the clock face, the forty-five was changed to forty. If both players have forty, the first player to score receives ten and that moves the clock to fifty. If the player scores a second time before the opponent is able to score, they are awarded another ten and the clock moves to sixty. However, if a player fails to score twice in a row, then the clock would move back to forty to establish another "deuce."

Another theory is that the scoring nomenclature came from the French game jeu de paume (a precursor to tennis, which initially used the hand instead of a racket). Jeu de paume was very popular before the French Revolution, with more than one thousand courts in Paris alone. The traditional court was ninety feet in total, with forty-five feet on each side. When the server scored, he moved forward fifteen feet. If he scored again, he would move another fifteen feet. If he scored a third time, he could only move ten feet closer.

The origin of the use of "love" for zero is also disputed. It's possible that it derives from the French expression for "the egg" (l'œuf) because an egg looks like the number zero. This is similar to the origin of the term "duck" in cricket, supposedly from "duck's egg," referring to a batsman who has been called out without completing a run. One possibility comes from the Dutch expression *iets voor lof doen*, which means to do something for praise, implying no monetary stakes. Another theory on the origins of the use of "love" comes from the acceptance that, at the start of any match, when scores are at zero, players still have "love for each other."

This last theory seems entirely ridiculous.

The man never played tennis as a young man but thinks he might like to pick it up as a hobby. There are courts nearby, and whenever he sees people out there playing, he thinks he might like to himself.

It's doubtful he will ever buy a racket, let alone play tennis with other people.

The man says, It may've been my wife.
The friend says, What may've been your wife?
The man says, That coaxed me into the water.
The friend says, You don't remember?
The man says, I'm trying.
The friend says, How can you not remember something like that?
The man says, It's a problem.

The man is conflating two events again, as he often does.

The day he almost drowned in the river took place a full week before a major catastrophe altered the lives of everyone in the community.

Two terrorists blew up a bus in the middle of morning rush hour, killing several and wounding dozens.

There is a memorial at the site of the explosion, commemorating those lost.

This day, there were several bystanders, many of whom were wounded. One, a twelve-year-old boy driving a bicycle on the sidewalk, succumbed to his wounds a week later. He became something of a poster child.

The man almost drowned in the river a week before all of this happened.

Why it comes to mind is that he drove right by the site on his way to the river. Of course, he only remembered this in retrospect.

It is true the man was coaxed into the river, and it was the woman who was about to go away who did the coaxing.

At this point, though, the man didn't know the woman was about to go away. He learned this months later, or perhaps it was years.

The man always has a hard time with chronology.

The woman going away, who coaxed him into the river, grew up in Poland or Romania or even Slovakia.

She spoke several languages and the man was impressed by this.

They were meeting one of her Polish friends, who had a German boyfriend who had a boat. The four of them were to go boating up and down the river.

They had coolers filled with beer and soda and sandwiches.

At one point the women stripped off their outerwear, revealing blue bathing suits.

One was in a one-piece and the other a bikini.

It's not important which was which.

Let's say for now that the woman who was about to go away was in the one-piece, as she was always modest.

The man watched the two Polish women swimming in the river. They were laughing and splashing and having a grand time.

This is when the woman who was about to go away coaxed the man into the water.

She said, Come on in with us.
He said, The water looks dirty.
She said, It's fine.
He said, I didn't bring my trunks.
She said, You have on boxers, yes?

At this point, the other Polish woman joined her friend in coaxing the man into the river.

The man hadn't swum in over twenty years and had never tried swimming in a river.

The man thought nothing of it, though. He thought it must be like riding a bicycle, which is another thing the man hadn't done in twenty years.

The man jumped in and started drowning at once.

He had never experienced a current before and it immediately pulled him down and away from the boat.

The man tried to remember what swimming entailed, the various motions of the arms and legs. There was awkwardness, confusion, frustration.

The man couldn't remember anything.

Nothing went through the man's mind as he started to drown. There were no memories, no regrets, no thoughts at all other than trying to remember how to swim.

Of course, the man was terrified during this time, which lasted five seconds or years.

The man would've drowned had the woman who was about to go away not dog-paddled over to rescue him. She came up and under him, hooking his arms with her own, and dragged him to the surface. Then she paddled over to the boat and helped him in.

Neither said a word as the man gasped for breath on the deck.

They were both trying to be nonchalant.

It's unclear if the Polish woman still in the water or the German piloting the boat were aware of what had happened.

No one said anything about it for the rest of the afternoon.

The woman immediately returned to the river once the man caught his breath.

He thought this was somewhat callous of her, but he was grateful she saved his life at the same time.

Of course, had she not coaxed him into the water, his life wouldn't have needed saving.

This made the man think of something his father used to tell him: that you should never bang your head against the wall just because it feels good when you stop.

Percy Bysshe Shelly, Gilbert of Gilbert and Sullivan, J.J. Astor and Benjamin Guggenheim, Grigori Rasputin, Hart Crane, Virginia Woolf, Arky Vaughan, Mary Jo Kopechne, Josef Mengele, Natalie Wood, Jeff Buckley, Spalding Gray, and Rodney King all drowned.

The friend says, Sometimes I get on a bus.
The man says, When?
The friend says, During the day.
The man says, I thought we were talking about drowning.
The friend says, I thought we were finished. Do you have anything to add?
The man says, I don't recommend it.
The friend says, Neither do I.
The man says, I thought you said you didn't take the bus.
The friend says, I never take the bus two blocks from my house.
The man says, You take another bus, then.
The friend says, Yes.
The man says, What goes on there?
The friend says, You wouldn't believe it.

The man says, Tell me.

The friend says, The dregs, the rabble.

The man says, Dregs and rabble.

The friend says, Robots, zombies.

The man says, So, that's how it is on the bus.

The friend says, This is it. This is how it works.

The man says, I always wondered.

The man has never wondered what it was like on a bus. The man has contemplated or speculated about a great many things, but never this.

Sometimes the man will say something in conversation that's intended to be funny or keep the conversation moving.

The man remembers dinner last night at the Italian restaurant his wife's new nudist friend recommended. He considers telling his friend about the dinner, but thinks better of it.

The friend was well acquainted with his wife's nudist friend and in fact had some kind of dalliance with her last year, before he met his wife, Janice.

Dinner was at a restaurant not far from where the man works. He'd walked past this restaurant many times and never realized it was there. The man never looks around or pays attention when he's out walking in the world. There is too much information to retain, he's decided—too many buildings and offices and restaurants and shops and none have anything to do with him. This is why he tries to keep his head down at all times, so he doesn't have to know anything that doesn't pertain to him.

He enjoyed his meal and so did his wife. They ate and drank and talked as they have countless times before. The food was good, as was the service. There were many others in the restaurant eating and drinking and talking. The man did not pay attention to any of them and they paid no attention to him, either.

One couple two tables over was discussing the conditions of their divorce. They wanted to handle this on their own, like adults. They didn't want to involve lawyers. They didn't want this to be acrimonious. One of them said Surely there has to be and the other said I couldn't agree more. There was awkwardness, confusion, frustration. From the beginning the man did what he was told, what he thought was right, and the woman resented him for this. Or else it was the other way around.

They did the math right there at the table. One of them said I'm not sure we can make this work. The other said Maybe we should stay together.

So they decided to try one last time.

The next morning one of them packed an overnight bag and left the country. This one left a note on the kitchen table that said, You can't argue with the math.

The one that left did fulfill certain dreams but never could shake a feeling of restlessness, a feeling that something was left undone.

The one that stayed behind barely noticed a change in his or her life. There was the continuing struggle to pay bills and the subsequent career changes, five times in four years.

The one that left died years later in a train accident somewhere in South America. The one that stayed behind learned about this through an old friend one night over dinner at this very same restaurant. They were there for the seafood, especially the mussels, which were supposed to be outstanding.

The mussels were from Prince Edward Island, a province of Canada.

The province currently accounts for a third of Canada's total potato production, producing approximately 1.3 billion kilograms annually.

Comparatively, the state of Idaho produces approximately 6.2 billion kilograms annually, with a population approximately 9.5 times greater.

This math doesn't seem to add up, either.

This night both the man and woman ordered the mussels and enjoyed them.

The one that stayed behind tried to feel something upon hearing this news, but couldn't summon any kind of reaction.

At the table next to this couple, a man said, I would like to compare this experience to some other experience, something I've done before, some common human endeavor to provide context or perspective, if only for myself, so I can better understand why I subjected myself to this, but I seem incapable of such things. I've given it an honest effort, I have, but I think it's beyond me.

His companion looked broken, done in. It was like her face and the rest of her body were paralyzed.

A woman sitting at the bar said, Inside the house I never make coffee, let alone drink it.

The man and woman didn't hear any of this and have never nor will ever be in the same room with these people again.

The man says, Do you talk to them?

The friend says, Talk to who?

The man says, The people on the bus.

The friend says, Hell no.

The man says, Not even once? As an experiment?

The friend says, I never talk to them and never will. I try to think about what's happened to my life and why it's happened. I'm afraid I can't account for any of it.

The man says, That's probably a good thing.

The friend says, How do you figure?

The man says, Suppose something happened because some other thing happened before that. Say that everything is causal or contingent upon sequence. Say you are determined to learn from these prior experiences so as not to repeat the same mistakes over again, the same patterns. But you are going to repeat the same mistake again. It's inevitable. We're all doomed in this regard.

The friend says, You're probably right.

The man says, So this happened and then that happened as a result, and where the hell are you?

The friend says, Nowhere.

The man says, Exactly.

The fly has not had the strength to venture out from behind the curtain today. It buzzes frantically every few minutes, knocking against the glass.

The friend says, What time is it?

The man looks at his watch.

Both men could look over to the stove, which features a clock, but neither does.

The man says, It's four thirty.
The friend says, Are we still having dinner later?
The man says, I do believe.
The friend says, Your wife hasn't changed her mind?
The man says, I don't think so, no.
The friend says, If it's going to be a problem....
The man says, I think it'll be fine.

The man told his friend that the woman is looking forward to having him for dinner, though everyone knows this isn't true.

The friend removes a toothpick from his mouth and rolls it between his fingers. He then places it on the table in front of him.

Both the man and woman refer to the stove as a stove. Neither knows the difference between stove and oven. Neither calls it a range.

The friend says, Where is she now?
The man says, I don't know.

There is quiet. Both men are thinking.

They take drinks from beer and whiskey.

The man says, No, I remember now. She is at an engagement party, I think. Someone she used to work with. A woman.
The friend says, I think they call it a shower.
The man says, I thought that was for babies. The friend says, I think it's for both.
The man says, It's all the same.
The friend says, Everything spills all over everything.
The man says, You shaved your beard.
The friend says, I shaved it a couple of days ago.

The man says, You look clean.
The friend says, I feel clean.
The man says, You're a handsome man either way.

The woman is at an engagement party. In fact, she is at the engagement party of the former colleague who adopted their first dog, Georgia.

The woman was surprised to be invited. She was under the impression her former colleague had moved away.

Indeed, her former colleague had moved to the Pacific Northwest and lived there for years.

Apparently things didn't work out, and she moved back two years ago, unbeknownst to the woman.

It turns out Georgia contracted distemper while out in the Pacific Northwest and had to be put down.

Distemper is a viral disease that affects various animals. It is a single-stranded RNA virus of the family paramyxoviridae, and thus a close relative of measles and rinderpest. Despite extensive vaccination in many regions, it remains a major disease of dogs.

Distemper isn't generally fatal, at least not in the early stages, but her former colleague was looking for an excuse to put the dog down and did so two days after the diagnosis.

The friend says, Usually I let my beard grow from Thanksgiving through Christmas.
The man says, I know this.
The friend says, Almost no one likes me with a beard, including Janice.

The man says, That's surprising to me.

The friend says, How so?

The man says, Women like beards.

The friend says, Not all of them.

The man says, I suppose that's true.

The friend says, It's my once-a-year protest.

The man says, What are you protesting?

The friend says, You name it.

The man says, My wife protests certain outrages.

The friend says, It's what I like most about her.

The man says, But you, my friend.

The friend says, I do what I can.

The man says, That's all you can do.

The friend says, They say with a beard I look like my father.

The man says, Your father is still alive?

The friend says, I think so. He's old, nearly dead.

The man says, So is mine.

The friend says, He used to do what he could but he can't anymore. His life is such that each day seems entirely uncalled for, a blow below the belt.

The man says, I thought your father was dead.

The friend says, His beard is always well groomed, whereas mine is scraggly and unkempt.

The man says, Even still.

The friend says, At Christmas, I refuse to accept or distribute gifts of any sort, even cards. I got this from him.

The man says, It's a sound practice.

The friend says, To family functions I wear the same flannel shirts, blue work pants tied with a rope around the waist, black shoes and white socks. I think of it as an homage and my father always gets a kick out of it. The others, though, they think I do it to mock him.

The man says, Homage is a great word. O mahhzzzzzhe. It's probably Latin or Greek.

The friend says, Jesus, his face looks like a cauliflower, it looks like it will slide clear off his skull. But his silver beard is still handsome. He is dignified.

The friend does resemble his father. People have commented on this resemblance his whole life. However, he's never worn flannel shirts and blue work pants to a family function.

The men toast dignity. They raise their glasses and say *dignity* out loud.

The friend says, When my father sees me, he pats my head, then cups my hairy chin with both hands. He has old man's hands. Do you remember those?
The man says, No.
The friend says, When you were a kid and you stayed in the bath too long and your hands got wrinkled.
The man says, Yes.
The friend says, The people in the family rarely have anything to say to either of us. One of the ancients, an aunt, sister to my father, she says I look like a terrorist. To my father and me, it is no such matter.
The man says, I can never grow a beard. It itches.
The friend says, You wouldn't look good with a beard.
The man says, That's what my wife says, too.
The friend says, There's no point arguing.
The man says, There is no point arguing. This is what I base my life on. I don't have a philosophy, but if I did it would be this.
The friend says, A life spent not bothering anyone is a life well spent. That is my philosophy, if I had one.

In addition to flies, they also have a problem with mosquitoes.

Both the man and woman have woken to find bites on their arms, heads, necks, faces, back and shoulders, feet and legs.

They sometimes try to lure mosquitoes into certain areas to kill them. They lie back on a sofa and exhale.

The woman is the one who told the man this, that mosquitoes are attracted to carbon dioxide.

He always thought it was blood.

The man and woman sometimes wear repellent to bed. They've also burned citronella candles.

Someone suggested mosquito netting to hang over the bed. The person said, It's not only for the Third World.

It's unclear if this was supposed to be funny.

The man has killed dozens of mosquitoes in the past several years and there are still bloodstains on certain walls.

The man says, I don't approve of the word *philosophy* when people say, in my philosophy. People don't have their own philosophies. They have everyone else's.
The friend says, There's no point arguing.
The man says, Except to say, you are full of shit, my friend.
The friend says, How do you figure?
The man says, You bother everyone.
The friend says, I can't help it sometimes.
The man says, You're human.
The friend says, There is that, after all.

The car parked outside resembles the first car the man ever owned, right down to the crack on the windshield. The crack looked like an intricate spider web with berserk lines going this way and that.

The man's first car would shake while in reverse. The man didn't realize this when he bought the car and reasoned that reverse was only important in certain situations and could be avoided to a large degree. One could not keep the car in reverse for long, though. Also, reverse was difficult to negotiate due to the car's poor handling. One could turn the steering wheel forty-five degrees without the tires reacting.

The brake pedal had to be depressed fully for the brakes to be activated. One did not necessarily have to slam the brakes to stop the car but one did have to apply a certain pressure. The braking distance was likewise appalling.

The man can't tell if this car has had similar problems, but it certainly looks like it.

The brakes squeaked when applied and his car made a knocking sound when turning right, which turned out to be the axle. There were holes in it. A mechanic informed the man of this. He has never known anything about cars and has no interest in cars.

The mechanic pointed out the holes while the car was on the lift in his shop. The man couldn't tell where the mechanic was pointing, couldn't identify the axle itself, let alone any holes in it. He asked if the holes would hinder the car's performance and the mechanic said the axle could hold out a while longer but would eventually need replacing. At some point, the car would become dangerous to drive.

This never happened.

The car died on its own before it had a chance to become dangerous.

Which isn't to say the man ever felt entirely safe driving the car.

He almost got into several accidents and always felt as if it were only a matter of time.

He once narrowly avoided a major accident by slamming on the brakes and making a hard right turn in the middle of a busy intersection.

Mary Ward, a scientist, was the first person killed by a motor vehicle. The accident occurred in Ireland in 1869, when she fell under the wheels of an experimental steam car built by her cousins.

Bridget Driscoll was the first pedestrian victim of an automobile collision, which occurred in 1896 in Great Britain. As she and her teenage daughter May and her friend Elizabeth Murphy crossed Dolphin Terrace in the grounds of Crystal Palace in London, Driscoll was struck by an automobile, belonging to the Anglo-French Motor Company, that was being used to give demonstration rides. One witness, a bystander, described the car as traveling at "a reckless pace, in fact, like a fire engine."

On September 13, 1899, Henry Bliss was the first American killed in a car accident. He was disembarking from a streetcar at West 74th Street and Central Park West in New York City when an electric-powered taxicab struck him and crushed his head and chest. He died from his injuries the next morning.

Arthur Smith, the driver of the taxicab, was arrested and charged with manslaughter but was acquitted on multiple grounds, including the absence of malice and negligence.

The man imagines himself getting hit by car whenever he crosses a street. He cannot tell if this is some kind of premonition or if it speaks to some sort of psychological issue.

The man says, And your father has been dead for years.

The friend says, He was a bastard, a good-for-nothing.

The man says, When my wife's angry that's what she calls me, a good-for-nothing.

The friend says, I'm sure she says the same about me.

The man says, Worse. She says worse about you.

The friend says, I am worse.

The man says, Well, some people are only good for one thing.

The friend says, Some even less.

The man says, You can't argue.

The friend says, She's not wrong.

The man says, Should we have another? Get a jump on the evening?

The friend says, I won't stop you.

The man walks over to the refrigerator to retrieve the soda, opens the freezer door and pulls out a bucket of ice, which he carries to the table.

The friend removes a toothpick from his mouth and places it on the table.

The friend says, I think Janice is getting worse.

The man says, We're all getting worse.

The friend says, Three times I've heard Janice talking to herself. Once during the news, once during a baseball game, and once during something else.

The man says, My wife always talks to herself. Women do this.

The friend says, I was in the den each time looking out the window. From the den, I can look out on that open field where the neighborhood kids play football.

The man says, Any prospects out there?

The friend says, From the den you can hear what's going on in the bathroom. Water running, cabinets opening and closing, things of this nature. Each time it sounded like mumbling.

The man says, Women mumble.

The friend says, So you don't think she's getting worse, then?

The man says, You know my position.

The friend says, Fuck you and your position.

The man says, She's a free spirit. You knew this about her.

The friend says, I knew nothing.

The man thinks of his wife as something of a free spirit, but she isn't.

He thinks of her friends as free spirits, too, but they're not.

The friend says, Last year at this time we were on our honeymoon in Ireland. She talked about opening a bed and breakfast. She said it would keep us busy. She said I couldn't go on taking disability and doing nothing for the rest of my life. She wanted us to look into it when we got back home.

The man says, People say things like that on vacation. It means nothing.

The friend says, Now she wants to go to the zoo. She mentioned it at dinner a few nights ago. We were having fish. She calls it brain food.

The man says, I think you're being too critical, if you ask me.

The friend says, But you understand what I'm talking about.

The man says, I'm afraid I understand very little.

The friend says, She said we haven't been to the zoo in years.

The man says, Is that true?

The friend says, We've never been to the zoo, certainly not together. Not even once. It's been never since we've been to the zoo.

The man says, This is a tough one.

The friend says, I think sometimes she has me confused with someone else.

The man says, That's possible. You are rather average in most respects.

The friend says, I don't dispute this.

The man says, It's indisputable.

The friend says, It's fucked, is what it is.

The man says, The zoo is fucked?

The friend says, I asked her, what's at the zoo? You know what she said?

The man says, What?

The friend says, Animals.

The man says, Animals.

The friend says, How do you respond to that?

The man says, She's a free spirit, you knew this.

There is most definitely something wrong with the friend's wife, Janice, but it's unclear what. She is reluctant to visit doctors, as she believes doctors were responsible for her sister's death. The doctors failed to detect an easily treatable heart condition that led to her sister's premature demise.

For one thing, Janice cannot sit still. She is forever flexing her arms and legs and cracking her joints. These noises bother the man but he hasn't pointed this out to his friend.

It seems as if she is aphasic at times. She often struggles for commonplace words and phrases. The man suspects she might suffer from dementia, but he isn't sure if this is possible in someone as young as Janice.

He thinks maybe she's done a lot of drugs and this is what's happened to her, the fallout, the aftermath.

Aphasia is a disturbance of the comprehension and formulation of language caused by dysfunction in specific brain regions. This class of language disorder ranges from having difficulty remembering words to losing the ability to speak, read, or write. Aphasia is usually linked to brain damage, most commonly by stroke. Brain damage linked to aphasia can also cause further brain diseases such as cancer, epilepsy, and Alzheimer's.

Conversely, dementia is a serious loss of global cognitive ability in a previously unimpaired person, beyond what might be expected from normal aging. It may be static, the result of a unique global brain injury, or progressive, resulting in long-term decline due to damage or disease in the body. Although dementia is far more common in the geriatric population, it can occur before the age of sixty-five, in which case it is termed early onset dementia.

Perhaps Janice is demented, but it's not likely.

The man does like to think in these kinds of dramatic terms, though.

For instance, during the four or five years that these two lost track of each other, the man would say out loud to his wife, He's dead to me, whenever his friend's name was invoked.

What seems more likely is that Janice has suffered some kind of mini stroke, also known as a TIA, or transient ischemic attack.

The man knows about this because his father, Jasper, suffered a mini stroke last year.

The only consequence of such has been a change in diet and various new medications, including blood thinners.

The friend says, Sometimes I think about taking off.

The man says, Where would you go?

The friend says, Somewhere else.

The man says, I don't like to see that sort of thing.

The friend says, It has nothing to do with you.

The man says, I'd rather not see it, that's all I'm saying.

The friend says, You didn't mind seeing it last week.

The man says, I don't think I had a choice.

The friend says, I didn't know that was going to happen.

The man says, Janice didn't mention anything? She didn't say…

The friend says, No, I was as surprised as you.

The man says, These things happen. It means nothing.

The friend says, There's no point arguing.

The two men are referring to what took place last weekend.

The man was over for a few beers and to watch the baseball game.

They watched as the local team put forth another embarrassing effort, a putrid display of what barely resembled major league baseball.

Janice was out with friends doing god knows what. She'd be home late.

The men watched the game and drank and spoke as men do the world over.

They discussed the first baseman's recent struggles and how it was indicative of a greater problem.

They talked about the car parked outside of the man's house. They talked about their wives and colleagues and medical conditions.

Janice returned home earlier than expected, announcing herself as she barged through the front door.

The game was in the eighth inning but had already been decided.

After a few pleasantries, Janice put on some music and started to dance. She said she wasn't finished having fun for the night.

This is when she started removing her clothes, which consisted of a sundress and undergarments.

She carefully folded each item and draped them over the credenza.

The man considered excusing himself but decided against it. He didn't want to seem rude or unappreciative.

It seemed as if this performance was intended for both him and his friend.

The man looked over at his friend, who was enjoying his wife's performance.

Before long, she was naked, and she danced liked this for a few minutes or hours.

Then she moved over to her husband and danced in his lap.

The man was both grateful for and disappointed by this. He drank from his beer.

The music kept playing. The man didn't recognize any of the songs.

On the television, the first baseman took a called third strike, a fastball on the inside corner.

By the time the first baseman was walking back to the dugout, Janice was kneeling in front of her husband.

The man didn't look away. He saw her go through the motions, up and down.

By the time the first baseman took his position for the top of the ninth, they were finished.

Janice turned to the man and said goodnight. She walked upstairs.

The man kept his eyes on the game so that his friend could put himself away.

Neither said anything and the evening concluded shortly after the game did.

On the way home, the man wanted to compare this experience to some other experience, something he'd done before, some common human endeavor to provide context or perspective, if only for himself but also perhaps his wife, should he decide to tell her, so he could better understand why he subjected himself to this, why this happened, what it said about all of them, but he was incapable of such.

The friend says, This morning we were on the porch, the two of us. We were having coffee. A flock of starlings were flying from tree to tree and lawn to lawn. Janice was staring at them. She was mesmerized, in a trance. Then finally she said, Would you look at that.
The man says, And this means...
The friend says, It was the way she said it.
The man says, With my wife, it was a flock of seagulls.
The friend says, What seagulls?

The man says, She was telling me a story about seagulls and how she saved one once.

The friend says, That's a nice thing to do.

The man says, This morning she was lying in bed and watching them fly outside the window. She said sometimes they fly and sometimes they float.

The friend says, What does that mean?

The man says, I don't know.

The friend says, It means something.

The man says, That's what I said. I said there was a double meaning, but she said there wasn't.

The friend says, There's definitely a double meaning.

The man says, There's no point arguing.

The friend says, I hate seagulls.

The man says, They are nasty creatures.

The friend says, I tried throwing a football at one once. Almost got it.

The man says, You always had a good arm.

The friend says, I'd like to go out there and join them.

The man says, Join who?

The friend says, The kids playing football.

The man says, It's not football season.

The friend says, I can wait till winter.

The man says, Football in the cold, in the snow.

The friend says, There's nothing better.

The man says, Let me know and I'll join you.

The friend says, I want to see my breath disappear in the air and lose sensation in my limbs. I want to go out for a pass and scream bloody murder when the ball hits me in the chest. I want to fall to the ground, desperate for wind. I want the other players to huddle over me. I want there to be genuine concern. I want to limp home after the game and feel sore. I want to take off my sweatshirt and leave it on the sofa to dry. How come something like this can't happen?

The man says, Because you married a folder.

The friend thinks about this, the implications. He wonders what his wife, Janice, might be folding this very minute.

She is at home, alone. She said she needed a day to rest her body, mind, and soul.

She is the kind of person who says such things out loud.

The man says, So, what was wrong with the starlings?

The friend says, It was like it was new to her, like she'd never seen a flock of starlings before.

The man says, Maybe she hasn't.

The friend says, Those starlings are always out there.

The man says, But maybe she didn't notice them. Not everyone sees the same thing. We were just talking about this very thing this morning.

The friend says, Who was?

The man says, My wife and I.

The friend says, That's fine.

The man says, Maybe she was oblivious to the starlings. This happens to people. It's like they have blinders on. You walk along a street and come to a tree.

The friend says, Fuck you and the tree.

The man says, Nobody looks around, has their eyes open. No one notices the tree. Sees it for what it is. You walk down the street and everyone is looking down. I've always wanted to know, what the hell are people looking at? What the hell is so fascinating about your own footsteps or the ground in front of you?

The friend says, Maybe they don't want to step on anything. Maybe they don't want to trip and fall. Maybe they don't want to go all back full and pull a muscle.

The man says, No one makes eye contact with a passing stranger. No one smiles. No one acknowledges other people.

The friend says, We've agreed to this, we've said don't look up. Looking up gets you in trouble. This is our philosophy. Do you not remember?

The man says, There's no point arguing.

The man thinks about his wife. He can't remember when she said she'd be home.

The man watches his friend play with the toothpick in his mouth, moving it from side to side. The man has never seen his friend pick his teeth, but he has seen him clean his fingernails with a toothpick. The man is equally repelled and fascinated by this action.

The friend says, But maybe we need to get into some trouble once in a while. To reassert our humanity, if nothing else.

The man says, You think so?

The friend says, I don't know.

The man says, Getting into trouble is another way we get into trouble.

The friend says, Can't argue with that.

The man says, But, then again.

The friend says, That's what I think.

The man says, Otherwise, it's all the same. Every day.

The friend says, I have no trouble not looking people in the eye.

The man says, Especially on the bus, I imagine.

The friend says, Especially there.

The last time the friend took the bus he ran into someone he used to work with. This person was no one he'd wanted to run into. They said hello to each other. They asked after each other's families. One of them said We should get together for a drink sometime and the other said Good idea.

Neither meant what they'd said.

The man says, I was in the park yesterday.

The friend says, Who was talking about the park?

The man says, No one.

The friend says, I didn't think so.

The man says, But now I am talking about the park. This is how conversation works. It's called a transition.

The friend says, Fuck you and your transitions.

The man says, That door over there, it isn't locked from the outside.

The friend says, As long as the whiskey is here, I'm staying.

The man says, Then I will talk about the park.

The friend says, This is your house.

The man says, My wife was home, and sometimes when the two of us are home together it's…

The friend says, So you went to the park.

The man says, I found an empty bench under a tree for shade. There were people walking around, biking, skating, what have you. Then I see a man with a guitar case walking toward my bench.

The friend says, What kind of man?

The man says, What do you mean, what kind of man?

The friend says, Young man, old man, ugly man, fat man, dirty man…

The man says, He was in his fifties, I'd say. He was portly, but not rotund.

The friend says, What did you do?

The man says, I tried to steer him to another bench with my eyes. I was trying to communicate non-verbally, so, in this case, I was most definitely looking up. I was trying to appear unapproachable, very pointed eye contact.

The friend says, It didn't work.

The man says, It didn't work. The guitar man sat right next to me. He didn't ask, didn't make a gesture of any kind, he just sat down next to me.

The friend says, This kind of thing happens on the bus sometimes.

The man says, Then he started talking to me. He said, How are you this morning? He had a ridiculous accent. He sounded like a bad actor trying to sound Irish. I think maybe he was waiting for me to ask how he was.

The friend says, Of course he was.

The man says, That's how people are. They don't care how you are, they only want to tell you how they are. They can't wait to tell you the whole ugly story of themselves.

The friend says, If I didn't know you better, I'd say there was a double meaning here.

The man says, Fuck you and your double meanings.

The friend says, Fair enough.

The man says, Then he starts up with this phony brogue. He says, I couldn't be better this morning meself. He said, 'tis a beautiful day. 'Course I'm no spring chicken, not anymore, can't keep up with these youngins. Can't understand 'em either, to tell you the truth. More's the pity. Still, I'm grateful to be alive on a day like today, my friend.

During this reenactment, the man affects an Irish brogue himself.

The friend says, What a fucking disaster.

The man says, Then he said, I've been all over the world and it's no better or worse right here, right here on this bench with you today.

The friend says, He said that?

The man says, This is what he said. Then he said, when in Rome I did as the Carthaginians did.

The friend says, So, what did you say?

The man says, I didn't say anything. I was flabbergasted. He talked about Hannibal crossing the Alps on elephants. Then he started in on the Sherpas, the people living in the Himalayas. He said they were famous as mountain climbers.

The friend says, Where did he get Sherpas from?

The man says, I think it was the mountains, the Alps. I think maybe he thought the Alps and the Himalayas were the same thing.

The friend says, Maybe he's right. Maybe it's the same.

The man says, It's all the same, everything.

Ancient Carthage was a Semitic civilization centered on the Phoenician city-state of Carthage, located in North Africa on the Gulf of Tunis, outside of what is now Tunis, Tunisia. It was founded in 814 BCE. Originally a dependency of the Phoenician state of Tyre, Carthage gained independence around 650 BCE and established a hegemony over other Phoenician settlements throughout the Mediterranean, North Africa, and what is now Spain, which lasted until the end of the third century BCE. At the height of the city's prominence, it was a major hub of trade, with political influence extending over most of the western Mediterranean.

For much of its history, Carthage was in a constant state of struggle with the Greeks on Sicily and the Roman Republic, which led to a series of armed conflicts known as the Punic Wars. The city also had to deal with the volatile Berbers, the indigenous inhabitants of the area where Carthage was built. In 146 BCE, after the third and final Punic War, Carthage was destroyed and then occupied by Roman forces. Nearly all of the other Phoenician city-states and former Carthaginian dependencies fell into Roman hands from then on.

Hannibal is the most famous Carthaginian and considered one of the greatest military commanders of all time.

The Himalayas is a mountain range in Asia separating the plains of the Indian subcontinent from the Tibetan plateau.

The Himalayan range is home to some of the planet's highest peaks, including the highest, Mount Everest. The Himalayas have profoundly shaped the cultures of South Asia. Many Himalayan peaks are sacred in both Hinduism and Buddhism.

The Sherpas are an ethnic group from the most mountainous region of Nepal.

Sherpas are highly regarded as elite mountaineers and experts in their local terrain. They were invaluable to early explorers of the Himalayan region, serving as guides at the extreme altitudes of the peaks and passes in the region, particularly for expeditions to climb Mount Everest. Today, the term is often used by foreigners to refer to almost any guide or porter hired for mountaineering expeditions in the Himalayas, regardless of their ethnicity. Because of this usage, the term has become a slang byword for a guide or mentor in other situations.

Which means that not all sherpas are Sherpas.

The Alps are an entirely different mountain range located in Europe.

The man has no interest in visiting either the Alps or the Himalayas.

If he had to choose one, if a gun were put to his head, he'd choose the Alps, as he has no interest in visiting Asia.

The friend says, What happened next?
The man says, He said Mount Everest is the peak of the Himalayas.

The friend says, Jesus.

The man says, Then I said to him, I'm afraid I will have to leave soon.

The friend says, I bet you weren't actually afraid.

The man says, I wasn't, no.

The friend says, Did he say anything?

The man says, I think he was disappointed.

The friend says, He probably wanted to serenade you.

The man says, He did.

The friend says, What do you mean, he did?

The man says, He serenaded me. I wasn't going to mention it.

The friend says, What happened?

The man says, He opened his guitar case and pulled out his guitar.

The friend says, What a crisis.

The man says, It was frightening, yes. But, also, it was nice. He had a nice voice.

The friend says, Fuck him and his nice voice. That's not right, in the middle of the day like that, in broad daylight, you minding your own business.

The man says, I know.

The friend says, What did he sing?

The man says, He called it a thirty-minute song in three-quarter time.

The friend says, Was it that long? I should hope not.

The man says, It went something like, Hallelujah I'm a bum, hallelujah bum again.

The friend says, I remember that song.

The man says, So did I.

The friend says, Did he try to kiss you?

The man says, I don't feel like talking about it.

The guitar player didn't try to kiss the man.

The guitar player has never tried to kiss a man in his life, which has lasted a long fifty-three years, but probably won't last another.

The guitar player has been unwell of late. He's had problems with digestion. It's probably cancer.

He finished his song and looked over at the man, who reached into his pocket and gave him a dollar.

The guitar player remained on the bench for the rest of the day. He played his thirty-minute song in three-quarter time for anyone who would listen, making almost seven dollars.

Three-quarter time is also known as waltz time.

Waltz, probably deriving from German Ländler, is dance music in triple meter, and often written in time signature 3/4. A waltz typically sounds one chord per measure, and the accompaniment style particularly associated with the waltz is to play the root of the chord on the first beat, the upper notes on the second and third beats.

The name "waltz" comes from the German verb *walzen*, in turn taken from the Latin verb *volvere*, which describes the turning or rotating movement characteristic of the dance.

Although French writers have attempted to connect the waltz to the sixteenth-century volta, firm evidence connecting this Italian form to the earliest occurrence of "walzen," in the mid-eighteenth century, is lacking.

Classical composers traditionally supplied music for dancing when required, and Franz Schubert's waltzes were written for household dancing, without any pretense at being art music. However,

Frédéric Chopin's surviving eighteen waltzes, along with his mazurkas and polonaises, were clearly not intended for dance. They marked the adoption of the waltz and other dance forms as serious composition genres.

The First World War, which destroyed the Austro-Hungarian monarchy and the Viennese culture, brought the long period of the waltz's popularity to an end. European light music shifted from Vienna to Berlin, and compositions by composers such as Gustav Mahler, Igor Stravinsky, and William Walton treated the dance in a nostalgic or grotesque manner, as a thing of the past.

In a jazz context, "waltz" signifies any piece of music in 3/4 time, whether intended for dancing or not. Almost all jazz before 1955 was in duple meter. It was only after the "bop waltz" appeared in the early 1950s (such as Thelonious Monk's recording of "Carolina Moon" in 1952 and Sonny Rollins's "Valse Hot" in 1956) that triple meter became at all common in jazz.

Neither the man nor his friend is musical, so neither considers the history of waltz music, though sometime next year the man will hear a waltz on the radio, which may spark an interest.

They continue to speak in this manner for another hour or so, discussing what is wrong with people, with themselves, with their wives, until the friend decides to go home.

END of ACT II

ACT III

The setting remains the same, an ordinary kitchen with a table and chairs.

It is the same Sunday, now evening.

The man is setting the table, which has been cleared of the beer and whiskey bottles, for supper.

The woman is also setting the table.

They are walking back and forth between the cupboards and table, each time retrieving something new, dinner plates, salad plates, water glasses, forks, knives, spoons, napkins.

They are using cloth napkins today, as it is Sunday.

The man says, How was the thing earlier?
The woman says, The shower, it was fine.
The man says, Did you enjoy yourself?
The woman says, It was a shower. I wasn't expecting to enjoy myself.
The man says, I understand.
The woman says, There were women in suits. There was food. There were gifts. I found myself stealing away to the upstairs bathroom at one point, but, otherwise, it was fine.
The man says, What was the matter?
The woman says, I couldn't take it anymore.
The man says, What couldn't you take?

The woman says, I don't like watching someone I don't know opening gifts.

The man says, I thought you knew her. I thought she was a colleague.

The woman says, She was, years ago.

The man says, Why were you invited?

The woman says, I don't know.

The man says, Why did you go?

The woman says, To be polite.

The man says, What did you give her?

The woman says, A toaster.

The man says, Is that a good gift?

The woman says, What do I care?

The man says, Well, then.

The woman says, Do you remember Georgia, the dog?

The man says, The crazy one?

The woman says, This was the woman who took her off our hands.

The man says, Is that right?

The woman says, It is.

The man says, How is Georgia?

The woman says, She got sick and had to be put down last year.

The man says, That's terrible.

The woman says, Cancer.

The woman didn't give the bride-to-be a toaster, but rather a gift certificate to a local spa that has an excellent reputation for using all-natural products.

The spa's owner is a young woman from California. She has visited the woman for acupuncture several times to treat her carpal-tunnel syndrome, which has been debilitating.

She says, Women were laughing, sipping tea, eating gourmet cookies, and there was the bride-to-be, showcasing the ring for the throng. I couldn't take it.

He says, I wouldn't take it either.

She says, So there I was upstairs in the bathroom, smoking cigarettes. I was blowing smoke out of the window and flicking ash into the toilet. The sound it makes is a hissing, when it hits the water. You've got to try it sometime.

He says, A hissing?

She says, Go try it. It's a great sound.

The woman has tried to quit smoking many times. She has chewed the gum, worn the patch.

The man doesn't smoke.

Still, he fishes a cigarette out of the pack left on the kitchen counter and disappears upstairs.

The woman continues setting the table. She also stirs the pot.

The man has made a kind of chicken stew.

He prepared most of it while the woman was at the shower and before his friend came over.

First he rinsed the organic chicken breast and then seasoned it with salt, pepper, and thyme and baked it for twenty minutes at 350 degrees.

During this time, he chopped onions, garlic, carrots, red bell peppers, celery.

Then he threw the vegetables into a pot and sautéed them while systematically adding chicken broth, tomato paste, crushed tomatoes.

Then he shredded the chicken and added that.

The man returns to the kitchen.

He scratches his head and in doing so musses his hair, if he has hair, which he does, though it is both thinning and receding.

The man thinks of himself as a good cook, but he isn't.

A monkey could make what he makes.

He says, That is a great sound. I don't know why I've never tried that before.
She says, I told you.
He says, How long were you in there?
She says, In where?
He says, The bathroom.
She says, Maybe half an hour, maybe more. They didn't miss me. I could hear the throng laughing and carrying on downstairs. I didn't know too many of them. The whole time I was thinking it was bad form to be up in the bathroom smoking cigarettes and drinking imported beer, but then I decided I didn't care.
He says, Good decision.
She says, I'm good with decisions.
He says, When did you decide this?
She says, I don't know.
He says, Indecision is as good a word as decision, probably better.
She says, What time is he getting here?
He says, He should be here soon.
She says, Last time he was late.
He says, I don't remember last time.

She says, And where is his wife tonight?
He says, She's not feeling well.
She says, The poor darling.
He says, She's a free spirit.

The woman looks at the man and this goes on for a time.

The world outside is going on the same as ever. There is weather and people and animals.

One could imagine that the neighbors are out walking the dog or Sunday driving or protesting police brutality, as last week saw a young black man shot dead by a cop somewhere in the middle of the country.

Let's say for now the victim was a young black man, but next time he can be brown or white or some other color altogether. However, statistics show that the next victim is likely to be black, too, and also the one after that.

Police aren't always particular about who they shoot and kill.

This was a time when police regularly shot and killed people.

Statistics show the next victim will be male.

One could imagine there are slugs and birds and cars moving about the world, too.

One could imagine Janice at home doing God knows what.

One could imagine almost anything. And then what, is the question.

So what is another question.

The friend enters through the kitchen door. He is carrying two bottles of wine and sets them down on the counter. He walks across the kitchen to the table and sits down.

The man says, Look who's here.

The woman doesn't look. She continues stirring the pot.

The friend says, Getting here was a problem, I nearly ran out of gas.

The man walks over to the window and looks out of it.

The man says, You walked.
The friend says, I know. Listen. Two planes take off from the same airport, one right after the other. One crashes twenty minutes into the flight, killing all 228 souls on board. The other plane lands safely at its destination, where all 228 souls die intermittently over the course of the next fifty-seven years—car accidents, fires, heart attacks, cancer.
The man says, I know this one.
The friend says, I don't believe you do.

There is silence. The man is trying to remember this one.

The man says, Okay, I give up.
The friend says, Let's talk about something else, then.
The man says, Good idea.

The man opens a bottle of wine and pours three glasses.

He then walks through the dining room and into the living room. He looks at the window.

He retraces his steps to the kitchen.

He says, That car is still out there.

The friend says, Maybe you should call the police.

The man says, I think I will if it's still there come the end of the week.

The friend says, Then that's settled.

The woman says, How is your darling wife?

The friend says, She's better now, thanks.

The woman says, I'm sorry, was she unwell?

The friend says, I think so, yes.

The woman says, Give her my regards, the darling.

The friend says, Of course.

There is quiet. Everyone is unsure of themselves.

The friend says, They're filming midgets on the other side of town. No one knows who is doing the filming or why they're doing it on the other side of town, but that's where they're doing it.

The man says, What are you talking about?

The friend says, Midgets. They're filming them on the other side of town. In the gazebo.

The man says, No one believes this.

The friend says, That's fine.

No one is filming anybody on the other side of town. The friend saw a movie where one of the characters said this line in a pitch of excitement because he happened upon a film shoot and one of the actors was a dwarf.

The man enjoyed this and has been looking for an opportunity to use it in conversation.

Historically, the term *midget* was used to describe proportionate dwarfs; however, this term is now regarded as offensive and pejorative.

A typical defining characteristic of dwarfism is an adult height of less than four feet ten inches. Since those with dwarfism have such a wide range of physical characteristics, variations in individuals are identified by diagnosing and monitoring the underlying disorders.

Disproportionate dwarfism is characterized by one or more body parts being relatively large or small in comparison to those of an average-sized adult, with growth variations in specific areas being apparent. In cases of proportionate dwarfism, the body appears normally proportioned, but is unusually small.

The man is nowhere close to being a dwarf or midget, standing at five feet seven inches.

Still, his wife towers over him.

Antonio Gramsci, Eddie Gaedel, Alexander Pope, and Chick Webb were all dwarfs.

Gandhi, James Madison, Andrew Carnegie, Charlie Chaplin, Picasso, Voltaire, Beethoven, Genghis Khan, Sammy Davis Jr., John Keats, and Toulouse-Lautrec were all five foot four or shorter, all thought of as midgets by family and friends, strangers and acquaintances, bystanders and passersby.

The man says, My beautiful bride was at a shower today.
The friend says, Is that right?
The woman says, That is correct.

No one says anything. This goes on for minutes, hours, days.

Down the block, the neighbors with the dog are sitting down to supper, too.

This night they have ordered takeout Chinese food and had it delivered.

One or the other will feed the dog a dumpling and get scolded for doing so.

After, one will make a pass at the other while watching a game show on television. The other will say, What the fuck is wrong with you?

The woman never fed Jasper the dog any human food, though the man would occasionally sneak him a hamburger or hot dog during summer.

Eventually the dog developed cancer and had to be put down.

The man and woman were devastated and said Never again.

The friend says, I forgot to shower today.
The man says, There are worse things that could happen.

Again there is quiet. Again the conversation goes nowhere.

The friend says, Some of the worst things that happen happen because I forget how to breathe or I get lost. For instance, I am out walking. There are buildings and trees and dogs and the sound of my shoes on the pavement. I've always liked the sound of my shoes on the pavement.
The man says, I, too, like that sound.
The friend says, I am talking about the sound of my shoes on the pavement, Charlie Shoemaker. The sound of my shoes on the pavement is like no one else's shoes on no other pavement. I'm not talking about your shoes.
The man says, I realize this. I, too, like the sound of your shoes on the pavement. I have often noted its particular rhythm and music.

The men look at each other.

Sometimes they call each other Charlie, though neither is named Charlie.

It is often in conjunction with some object—like Charlie Beer Bottle, Charlie Ballgame.

Both enjoy the sound of shoes on pavement, on hardwood floors, any surface where a report is audible.

The friend says, Then like that I forget how to breathe. If I don't think about it, I'm fine. I can breathe like everyone else in the world if I don't think about it. But then I start to think about it.

The man says, This is troubling.

The friend says, Oftentimes I collapse right there on the street. My chest hurts and my vision blurs and my mouth goes dry and then I'm down.

The man says, Down on the ground.

The friend says, Only sometimes do I get the shakes when I am lying on the pavement.

The man says, The shakes are no good.

The friend says, People are careful to step around me whenever this happens. Sometimes people are good this way. But other times not so much. Sometimes they kick me when I'm flopping around on the pavement. The kicks hurt but sometimes it's like they are jump-starting the breathing, hard as that might be to believe.

The man says, Being outside is dangerous, with the people.

The friend says, Yes, they are always spilling onto me and everyone else. And this is why I like to stay in the house. I almost never forget how to breathe in the house. I never have any trouble when I am inside.

The woman says, This would be awful if it were true.

The friend says, It's true, I've been to the doctor.

The man says, It's true, he has.

The woman says, And what did the doctor say?

The friend says, They don't know anything.

The man says, It's true, they don't.

The friend says, The worst part is, I bruise easily so I always have black and blue bruises up and down my ribs. Both sides.

The woman says, Show them to me.

The friend says, I'm afraid I can't.

The woman says, Too shy, are you?

The friend says, I've always been modest.

The woman says, I've heard otherwise.

Everyone looks at everyone else.

The woman says, What about the toothpicks?

The man says, What about the toothpicks?

The woman says, Wouldn't you swallow them?

The friend says, Hasn't happened yet.

The friend has suffered from panic attacks, and during these he does forget to breathe. He doesn't realize he's holding his breath and by then it's too late. He hears a whooshing sound in his ears and he starts to pass out. When he comes to, he is gasping for breath.

No one has ever beaten him, though.

His wife, Janice, is responsible for most of the bruising.

She has a habit of kicking and punching in her sleep.

This sleep disorder is very rare and may be more common in smokers or those heavily exposed to pesticides.

The sleep-kicking disorder is actually called REM sleep behavior disorder. People typically lose muscle tone during the rapid eye movement stage of sleep, but this doesn't occur in people with the disorder, causing movements that can seriously harm the individual or their sleep partner. It is estimated to affect only 0.5 percent of adults.

Parkinson's patients have been known to start acting out in their dreams, often punching or kicking the person sharing their bed.

Parkinson's disease is best known for its physical symptoms, like slowness and tremor, but is often preceded by a host of seemingly unrelated symptoms like mood change, loss of smell, constipation, and sleep disorders. Problems with thinking and memory are also common in Parkinson's disease, with patients being six times more likely to be diagnosed with dementia.

This might explain some of Janice's behaviors.

The man says, It's all the same, in the end. Is it not?
The woman says, What is?
The man says, Everything. Everything in the world is the same. Modesty, immodesty. Bruises up and down ribs. Strangers kicking you on the sidewalk. It's all the same. We are all on the same road here. This table is the same as a tree is the same as this glass is the same as all of us talking and busing and bruising and the same as a man fucking a tree or a car or a submarine slamming on the brakes.
The friend says, We call that all back full, in the business.
The woman says, There's something wrong with the lot of you.

There is quiet. Two of the three take sips of wine.

The friend says, Who was fucking a tree?
The man says, Joyce Kilmer.

The friend says, Never heard of her.

The man says, No one has.

The friend says, And this Joyce Kilmer fucks trees?

The man says, He used to. He's dead now. Some maple caught him with a sexy oak and bashed his skull in.

The friend says, So this Joyce is a man? The man says, He used to be.

The friend says, I don't like hearing about this.

Joyce Kilmer was an American writer and poet remembered primarily for a short poem titled "Trees."

Most critics disparaged Kilmer's work as being too simple, overly sentimental, and suggested that his style was far too traditional, even archaic.

He was killed by a sniper's bullet at the Second Battle of the Marne in 1918 at the age of thirty-one.

The Second Battle of the Marne was the last major German spring offensive on the Western Front during the First World War. The German attack failed when an Allied counterattack led by French forces and including several hundred tanks overwhelmed the Germans on their right flank, inflicting severe casualties. The German defeat marked the start of the relentless Allied advance, which culminated in the Armistice about one hundred days later. Thus the Second Battle of the Marne can be considered the beginning of the end of the Great War.

There is no evidence Joyce Kilmer ever had sexual relations with a tree or suffered from any paraphilia whatsoever.

The woman says, What about your darling wife?

The friend says, What about her?

The woman says, Seems like she would like this kind of repartee.
The friend says, I don't know about that.
The woman says, She's a free spirit, is she not?

It is quiet again. There is always a lot of air in a conversation between these three people.

There is time to think of other matters.

The man thinks about the car again, and how it reminds him of the first one he owned. That car's acceleration was poor, and while he never timed the car going from zero to sixty miles per hour, it probably took two to three minutes depending on the weather. When the temperature was below freezing, the car did not perform well. Warming the car up didn't seem to help, either.

Merging onto highways was tricky business, regardless of the weather. There had to be no cars in the intended lane for a successful merger. He almost caused several accidents merging onto highways.

There were a lot of things that didn't work; for instance, the speakers. There were only two speakers, located on the inside panels of the front doors. The speaker on the passenger side door cut in and out. There was probably a loose wire, a faulty connection somewhere, but the man never tried to get it fixed. The left blinker did not stop blinking unless the driver stopped it his or herself. The clicking sound that often accompanies indicators did not work, either. There were many occasions when he'd drive around for miles threatening a move left or right.

The passenger's side mirror was missing and the left front tire was perpetually in need of air, like an asthmatic, like his wife. The tire didn't struggle for breath or fumble with inhalers, of course.

The man is planning to go outside later and take a closer look at the car. He doesn't know what's inside of it. Perhaps there will be a clue of some sort.

A moth flies from one end of the kitchen to the other, toward the fluorescent light. The friend notices the moth but doesn't comment on it.

The friend says, I was watching the news before I came over.
The man says, What is the news of the day?
The friend says, It's raining. Everyone agrees on this.
The man says, It's collusion.
The woman says, It's not collusion, it's a consensus. There's a difference.
The friend says, There is, in fact, a difference here.
The woman says, Why do you look different?
The man says, He shaved his beard.
The woman says, That's right.
The man says, Does he not look handsome?

Janice likes to watch the news with her husband in the living room, but nowhere else. She will not watch the news in their bedroom or any other room. She doesn't want the news to infect those areas. So in the living room they will sit side by side on the sofa and watch. Her husband almost always takes the throw pillow and places it between them. He likes to prop his arm up on the pillow, ever since the accident. Janice stays on her side of the pillow when they watch the news. She likes to comment on the goings-on, what they're reporting. Her husband agrees with her by moving his head up and down.

The only time Janice has ever watched the news in her bedroom was in the wake of the terrorist attack ten years ago.

She was living alone then, with her two cats.

She stayed in bed and watched the news of those lost in the tragedy, including the twelve-year-old boy on his bicycle killed in the explosion.

She did this for three days straight, but hasn't done it since.

The cats lived long and healthy lives. One died of old age and the other ran away.

The woman does think the friend looks handsome but she will not say this aloud.

The woman says, I read today that a man was caught having sex with his car.
The friend says, How would you?
The man says, It's not important.
The friend says, It takes all kinds.
The woman says, That it does. Have you ever fucked a car?
The friend says, Not that I can recall, no.
The woman says, What about a tree? Have you ever fucked a tree?
The friend says, Perhaps once, in college.
The man says, It was probably a fall-down tree.
The friend says, What's a fall-down tree?
The woman says, It's a song.
The friend says, I don't know it.
The man says, Neither do I.
The woman says, This morning my husband said that people don't notice trees.
The friend says, That sounds like you.
The woman says, Do you notice trees?
The friend says, I can't say that I do.

The woman says, So trees go unnoticed around you, then.
The friend says, That's fair to say.
The man says, People don't look up. We know this.

The most recent hurricane, the one that had the woman volunteering in the park along with the neighbors, toppled over 8,000 trees in the city alone. Of course, it doesn't take a hurricane to uproot trees.

A young woman was killed by a falling branch during this most recent hurricane. She was out walking her dog.

Why she was out walking a dog in the middle of a hurricane is unclear.

All trees have the potential to fail at some level from force of wind, snow, or ice. One main reason, all tree experts agree, is the phenomenon known as windthrow, which uproots a tree. The tree trunk acts as a lever and so the force applied to the roots and trunk increases with height. Taller trees are more susceptible to windthrow.

The roots of trees can extend 1-2.5 times the radius of the branches, and many urban areas do not allow this extensive development. The problem lies mostly with trees that have been developed around and had roots cut, crushed, or torn in the process. There may be ensuing decay.

Wood is a strong structural material; however, it is not homogeneous or consistently strong at all places in the stem. Wood decay caused by fungi can weaken wood structure. However, the mere presence of decayed wood or even a hollow does not mean that the tree is more vulnerable to failure.

No one thinks of the thought experiment that asks if a tree falls in a forest and no one is there to hear it.

Which isn't to say that these three have never pondered the whys and wherefores of this question.

The man once spent an entire day in a forest, under a tree, thinking this question all the way through. He was only a boy, no more than eleven. He'd played baseball that day. He'd had a conversation about baseball with the mailman, Ben. He may've also had a conversation about baseball with his father. Sometimes he confuses the two.

Philosopher George Berkeley, in his work "A Treatise Concerning the Principles of Human Knowledge" (1710), proposes, "But, say you, surely there is nothing easier than for me to imagine trees, for instance, in a park and nobody by to perceive them. The objects of sense exist only when they are perceived; the trees therefore are in the garden...no longer than while there is somebody by to perceive them."

In June 1883, in the magazine *The Chautauquan*, the question was put, "If a tree were to fall on an island where there were no human beings, would there be any sound?" This is believed to be the first time anyone framed it so.

Albert Einstein is reported to have asked his fellow physicist and friend Niels Bohr, one of the founding fathers of quantum mechanics, whether he realistically believed that "the moon does not exist if nobody is looking at it." To this, Bohr replied that however hard he (Einstein) may try, he would not be able to prove that it does, thus giving the entire riddle the status of a kind of an infallible conjecture—one that cannot be either proved or disproved.

Both the man and his friend have come to similar conclusions, though neither has read Bohr.

The woman says, When should we eat?
The man says, I can wait.

The friend says, So can I. I had a late lunch.
The woman says, What did you have?
The friend says, Fish.
The man says, Brain food.

The friend cannot feel hunger but will eat when it's time to do so.

Outside, no one passes by, either on foot or in cars or buses. There are birds flying around out there, though, both seagulls and starlings.

Fish is indeed considered brain food, as it is a nootropic, which is a substance that enhances cognition and memory and facilitates learning.

Nootropics are thought to work by altering the availability of the brain's supply of neurochemicals by improving the brain's oxygen supply or by stimulating nerve growth.

The friend says, Speaking of modest…
The man says, What modest?
The friend says, From before. We were talking about modesty.
The man says, That's right.
The friend says, That friend of yours.
The woman says, What friend is this?
The friend says, Your friend, the nudist.
The woman says, The one you humiliated.
The friend says, I wouldn't go that far.
The woman says, You always go that far.
The man says, She's right, you do.

It's not clear if the friend ever humiliated the woman's nudist friend.

This episode is open to interpretation.

He did try to make a joke at a party in front of everyone one evening, but to him this wasn't at all humiliating.

And it certainly wasn't his intention to humiliate anyone.

He liked the nudist and enjoyed spending time with her.

The man agrees that what his friend said at the party in front of everyone wasn't at all an attempt to humiliate the nudist, but the woman does not.

The neighbors with the dog were at this particular party, though they left early to go home and feed the dog and as such didn't hear this humiliation or joke.

After they fed the dog that night, one made a pass at the other and the other responded by saying, Not again.

The man says, Some call nudism naturalism.
The woman says, What of it?
The man says, Nothing of it. I'm pointing it out.
The friend says, That's funny.

The man has spent hours on the Internet looking up nudism.

There is quiet. People take sips of wine. The man thinks to put out the cheese dish and some bread, but then forgets to do so.

The man says, I suppose it is natural. As nature intended. Mother Nature, nude for all to see. Naked trees and seagulls and starlings, men and women.
The woman says, This is tedious.
The man says, It's all the same. Naked, clothed, natural, unnatural. All the same.

The woman says, Who was talking about starlings?

The man says, He was, earlier. He had a problem with the starlings.

The woman says, What was your problem with the starlings?

The friend says, I didn't have a problem with the starlings. Charlie Birdman is mistaken.

The woman says, Is this true, Charlie Birdman? Are you mistaken?

The man says, It certainly is possible. I have been mistaken before. I probably make a great many mistakes during the course of a day.

The woman says, I should say so.

The man thinks of Charlie Parker, who was known as Bird and was a highly influential saxophonist, a leading figure in the advent and development of bebop.

The man likes jazz, but isn't particularly fond of Charlie Parker.

His wife, who played sax when she was younger and still practiced every so often until she developed asthma, considers Charlie Parker a god.

However, she doesn't think of Charlie Parker during this conversation and will not again until she hears "Yardbird Suite" on the car radio next month while commuting to work.

The man says, I have been mistaken for a tour guide. Whenever I am out and about, people ask me for directions. On the street, in the park, it's all the same.

The friend says, You look like you know where everything is.

The man says, I don't.

The friend says, I know. It's false advertising.

The woman says, It is. False advertising is no good.

The man says, I agree.

The man doesn't know where everything is. In fact, his sense of direction is poor, though it has improved over the years, marginally.

While the man does know from which direction the sun rises and sets, this knowledge has never been helpful when finding an address. He can never remember which streets/avenues run north-south and which go east-west. He only thinks in terms of forward and backward and everything looks the same to him regardless. There have been many occasions when he has been unable to find where it is he is supposed to go. This has happened to him on foot, while taking public transportation, and in his own cars.

Starlings are small to medium-sized passerine birds in the family Sturnidae. The name "Sturnidae" comes from the Latin word for starling, *sturnus*. Many Asian species, particularly the larger ones, are called mynas, and many African species are known as glossy starlings because of their iridescent plumage. Starlings are native to the Old World, from Europe, Asia, and Africa to northern Australia and the islands of the tropical Pacific. Several European and Asian species have been introduced to these areas, as well as North America, Hawaii, and New Zealand, where they generally compete for habitat with native birds and are considered to be invasive species. The starling species familiar to most people in Europe and North America is the common starling, and throughout much of Asia and the Pacific the common myna is indeed common.

The common starling is a noisy bird, especially in communal roosts and other gregarious situations, with an unmusical but varied song. Its gift for mimicry has been noted in literature, including the *Mabinogion* and the works of Pliny the Elder and William Shakespeare.

Unpaired males find a suitable cavity and begin to build nests in order to attract single females, often decorating the nest with ornaments such as flowers and fresh green material, which the female later disassembles upon accepting him as a mate. The amount of green material is not important, as long as some is present, but the presence of herbs in the decorative material appears to be significant in attracting a mate. The scent of plants such as yarrow acts as an olfactory attractant.

The nests are green, different shades of green.

Common starlings are both monogamous and polygamous; although broods are generally brought up by one male and one female, occasionally the pair may have an extra helper. Pairs may be part of a colony, in which case several other nests may occupy the same or nearby trees. Males may mate with a second female while the first is still on the nest. The reproductive success of the bird is poorer in the second nest than it is in the primary nest and is better when the male remains monogamous.

The friend says, Is there a double meaning here?
The man says, Who's to say?
The woman says, Words have meaning, friends. Actions have meaning. Some words have multiple meanings, multiple definitions. Some actions have multiple meanings, too.
The man says, There's no point arguing.
The woman says, Take nudism and naturism, for instance.
The man says, Let's take it for a walk around the block, for an ice cream.

The woman glares at the man.

She looks past and through.

The friend sees this but does not comment and in truth thinks nothing of it, as he's seen it before.

The man does like to take his wife for an ice cream at the local parlor. He'll say this to her if she seems blue in any way. He says, Come on, I'll take you for an ice cream.

The woman says, Some would say that being nude is natural. Some would say that it is unnatural to be in nude in public. Some would say that we are social creatures and that we do things in groups, in units, as a clan, a conclave, a pack. Like animals. In certain parts of the world, certain tribes all eat together and drink together and bathe together and they all go upstate together to cabins out in the wild together and they work together and play together and get naked and perform acts on each other together and sleep together and there are no distinctions made between any of these behaviors, but in other parts of the world this is not how people operate.

Again it is quiet. No one is enjoying themselves.

The man says, In certain parts of the world they speak incomprehensible languages. Grunts and groans, I tell you.
The friend says, I'm not sure I understand.
The woman says, I'm sure you don't.
The man says, I don't understand how people from other countries understand each other. Their languages.
The friend says, It's baffling.
The woman says, Excuse me.

The woman gets up from the table and leaves the kitchen. It's unclear if she's going upstairs to use the bathroom or what.

Naturism or nudism is a cultural and political movement practicing, advocating, and defending social nudity in private and in public. It may also refer to a lifestyle based on personal, family, and/or social nudism.

The man actually said naturalism, which isn't the same as naturism.

No one noticed his mistake.

Naturalism is the idea or belief that only natural, as opposed to supernatural or spiritual, laws and forces operate in the world—in other words, the idea or belief that nothing exists beyond the natural world.

Naturalism has nothing to do with nudity.

The naturist philosophy has several sources, many of which can be traced back to early twentieth century health and fitness philosophies in Germany, though the concepts of returning to nature and creating equality are also cited as inspiration. From Germany, the idea spread to the UK, Canada, the United States, and beyond, where a network of clubs developed.

The word naturism was used for the first time in 1778 by a French-speaking Belgian, Jean Baptiste Luc Planchon, and was advocated as a means of improving the natural style of life and health.

The usage and definition of these terms varies geographically and historically. Though in the United States, naturism and nudism have the same meaning, in Britain there is a clear distinction. Nudism is the act of being naked, while naturism is a lifestyle which at various times embraced nature, environment, respect for others, self-respect, crafts, healthy eating, vegetarianism, teetotalism, non-smoking, yoga, physical exercise, and pacifism as well as nudity.

The man and woman have never practiced nudism, per se, though they did go to a nude beach once together.

The woman removed her top but kept her bottoms on, while the man removed his bottoms and kept his top on.

The woman did this out of modesty, whereas the man didn't want to expose his chest to the sun.

The man has had a lifelong heat rash at the top of his chest.

The friend would go to clothing-optional beaches with a friend of his years ago, but always remained fully clothed.

That is to say, he wore bathing trunks.

The friend says, I couldn't understand my father. My own father. He had an accent. It was terrible.
The man says, The one with the beard and the hands?
The friend says, That's him, yes.
The man says, I'm sorry.
The friend says, He was a bastard. I had lunch with him once in an outdoor café somewhere near water. They served us pan-seared whatnots in a whatsoever sauce. I think it was good but I can't remember. The waitress was from Bulgaria. She didn't apologize. It was awful.
The man says, I don't understand.
The friend says, I don't, either. There's no shame in it. This is our problem right here. We seek understanding. We crave it, we want to touch it, hold it. But understanding doesn't want this. Understanding wants nothing to do with us.
The man says, I think you're right.
The friend says, The best we can do is….
The man says, We have to slow down. Speak clearly. Use our words.
The friend says, This is what I believe.
The man says, Use hand signals if necessary. Make ourselves as clear as possible so we stay out of trouble.
The friend says, I'm not sure it's possible.

The man says, True. It does seem futile, this attempt. We're all getting worse.

The man knew his friend's father and understood him perfectly.

That is to say, he understood the words, but the meanings or implications were often lost on him.

His friend's father didn't have an accent, but rather a peculiar way of pronouncing certain words that was nearly impossible to follow.

The woman returns and sits back down at the table. There's no telling where she went or what she did when she got there.

The man runs his fingers through his hair, which he still has, though not for long.

The man will be completely bald in about three years. What he chooses to do about it, if anything, is anyone's guess.

He is not the kind of man that will look good bald. His skull seems misaligned, misshaped. There are several planes and contours, certain protuberances, none of which seem like design.

Phrenology is a pseudoscience primarily focused on measurements of the human skull, based on the concept that the brain is the organ of the mind and that certain brain areas have localized, specific functions or modules. Developed by German physician Franz Joseph Gall in 1796, the discipline was very popular in the nineteenth century.

The man says, Earlier today he told me about his experiences on the bus. Dregs and rabble, he said. It was troubling.

The friend says, No place for women and children, this I can tell you.

The man says, It's always women and children first.

The friend says, What is?

The man says, When the ship is sinking. It's women and children first.

The friend says, First for what?

The man says, Fuck you first for what.

The friend says, How do you live with this man?

The woman says, I won't answer that question.

The friend says, It's always women and children first on the bus, too. First ones on, first ones off. First ones sitting, first ones standing. The bus is always filled with the women and children.

The man says, The women and their children, that sounds like a title for a movie. About someone cleaning a bathroom. What was it again?

The woman says, Now is not the time.

The friend says, What are you talking about?

The man says, She has an idea for a movie. It's about a bathroom.

The friend says, A thriller.

The woman says, I wouldn't think you'd find it thrilling. I would think other activities would be more thrilling for you. Even my husband said once that you were a thrill-seeker. I think he said the same about your darling wife, too.

The man did refer to his friend and Janice as thrill-seekers, but this is something of a misnomer.

A thrill-seeker is somebody who appears to be addicted to endogenous epinephrine. The high is caused by intentionally inducing a fight-or-flight response by engaging in stressful or risky behavior, which causes a release of epinephrine by the adrenal gland. Whether or not the positive response is caused specifically by epinephrine is difficult to determine, as endorphins are also released during the fight-or-flight response.

Typical thrill-seeking activities include skydiving, bungee jumping, certain kinds of whitewater rafting, running with the bulls.

The friend and his wife, Janice, aren't interested in these sorts of activities and haven't engaged in any.

The man cannot be characterized as a thrill-seeker, either.

He doesn't enjoy epinephrine or adrenalin or stimulants of any kind.

As a younger man, he was once talked into riding a roller coaster and he didn't enjoy the experience. In fact, he vowed never to step onto another for the rest of his life.

The woman who coaxed him into the roller coaster wasn't the same woman who coaxed him into the river where he nearly drowned.

However, these two women had a lot in common.

Both were going away soon, back to where they'd once belonged. Both had height and weight and lived daily lives.

They were women, like millions of others.

The woman says, In fact, those were his exact words, thrill-seekers. He said that you and your darling wife were thrill-seekers. Do you remember, Charlie Thrill-Seeker?
The man says, I'm afraid I don't.
The woman says, I do. I remember it well. You were out. You came home late. You were drunk. I was asleep. You woke me. You wanted sex. You were riled. You'd been riled. Then you said what you said about the thrill-seekers.
The man says, I'm afraid I don't remember.

The man does, of course, remember.

The man was over at the friend's house for a few beers and to watch the baseball game. It was their habit to get together like this every weekend. They enjoyed this tradition and thought of it as such, one of the few that either recognized or upheld.

They watched as the local team put forth another embarrassing effort, a putrid display of what only somewhat resembled major league baseball.

It could easily have been a football game, had it been football season, which it wasn't.

Janice was out with friends doing god knows what. She'd be home late.

Janice was, in fact, at a book club meeting, where they were discussing the virtues of a recently published novel and drinking wine. One woman, a librarian, argued that the novel was an allegory for contemporary America, wherein random acts of violence had become the norm. Almost everyone agreed with the librarian, including Janice, though she was most fond of the character named Genevieve.

She always liked the name Genevieve.

The men watched the game and drank and spoke as men do the world over.

Had it been football season, they'd have discussed the quarterback's recent struggles and how it was indicative of a greater problem. The quarterback lacked mobility and thus couldn't avoid the rush. He also didn't possess a strong arm and often couldn't throw a tight spiral, particularly if there was any wind or weather.

This day they dissected the problem with the right side of the infield.

They spoke of matters great and small.

They talked about the car parked outside of the man's house and speculated as to who might own it.

The friend had a theory that involved a young girl running away from an abusive husband.

Janice returned home earlier than expected, announcing herself as she barged through the front door.

She had, by herself, consumed a bottle and a half of Pinot Noir.

The game was still on but had already been decided.

After a few pleasantries, Janice put on some music and started to dance. She said she wasn't finished having fun for the night, though she didn't think the book club meeting was much fun.

She decided to join the book club because she was bored and felt isolated in her new marriage.

The truth is she doesn't enjoy reading books, but she likes getting out of the house once in a while and drinking wine and listening to the women talk.

She didn't read the whole book for this month's discussion and has no idea what book she'd suggest for next month, as it is her turn to pick.

This is when she started removing her clothes, which consisted of a business suit and undergarments.

She carefully folded each item and draped them over the credenza.

The man considered excusing himself but decided against it. He didn't want to seem rude or unappreciative, and he'd always thought Janice was attractive and wanted to see what she looked like naked.

He'd watched her bend over countless times and noted that she favored G-string underwear. This aroused him, as did her belly, which was pierced. She often bore her midriff and exposed her shoulders and legs.

It seemed as if this performance was intended for both him and his friend.

While she did focus most of her attention on her husband, she did look over to see if the man was watching. They made eye contact several times.

The man looked over at his friend, who was enjoying his wife's performance, but he was careful not to make eye contact. He was pretty sure his friend wouldn't look up and away from his wife.

Before long, she was naked, and she danced liked this for a few minutes or hours.

Then she moved over to her husband and danced in his lap.

The man was both grateful and disappointed by this. He was hoping she'd dance over his way and grind into him.

He'd heard of this sort of thing happening before.

He never considered the idea of swapping wives before this night, but the thought did cross his mind as he watched Janice dance. He drank from his beer.

The music kept playing. The man didn't recognize any of the songs, though one was a new release that sampled Charlie Parker's "How High the Moon."

On the television, the quarterback was picked off by a free safety, his third interception of the game.

By the time the quarterback was walking to the sidelines, Janice was kneeling in front of her husband.

The man didn't look away. He saw her go through the motions up and down on his friend and he took himself out of his pants and began doing likewise.

By the time the quarterback took the field for his next possession, everyone had finished.

Janice turned to the man and said goodnight. The man said goodnight back.

She walked upstairs naked.

The man kept his eyes on the game so his friend could put himself away.

The man had finished a couple of seconds before they did and so he'd already put himself away.

Neither said anything and the evening concluded shortly after the game did, which took another half hour and two beers.

The man got home and his wife was already in bed. He couldn't tell if she was asleep, so he stepped gingerly into the bedroom, but made a point to knock into the dresser.

He wanted sex.

He stripped off his clothes and jumped into bed.

His wife didn't stir.

The man maneuvered right up next to his wife, his erection poking her in the back.

He started kissing her neck, pulling her hair back as he did so. At first she said nothing; at first there was no discernible reaction to her husband's affections.

This sort of behavior wasn't without precedent, but it had been some time since the man had attempted this sort of maneuver in the middle of the night. Most often he'd fondle himself as a means to initiate some sort of sexual commingling.

She said, What's gotten into you?
He said, You wouldn't believe it.
She said, What?

The man told her what had happened at his friend's house.

He left out certain details pertaining to what he did during this episode.

He suggested they do something like this, together, as a group. He used the word swap.

The woman was appalled.

The man did not get to have sex that night.

Rather, the woman asked a series of questions. Some ended with, And you want that? Others ended with, And you watched?

The conversation went on for five minutes or years.

The woman said, I can't believe you.
The man said, What was I supposed to do?
The woman said, You have to be kidding me.
The man said, I'm sorry. It was a mistake.
The woman said, I can't believe you.

The man's erection subsided and didn't return until morning, when he woke and had to empty his bladder.

The woman says, Are you a thrill-seeker?
The man says, Now is not the time, dear.
The woman says, Well, if everything is the same and I think we've established that it is, then we can assume that now is, in fact, the time. Now is always the time. And because it's all the same, now is the same as later, so there you are.
The man says, This is interesting. Is time not an illusion, then? If now and later are indeed the same, then how can we differentiate between now and later?
The woman says, Fuck now and later.
The friend says, I don't feel well.
The woman says, Do you not feel well now? Because later you might feel better. Later my husband might fuck a tree or a car for us. He hasn't yet, but he probably wants to try.
The man says, Now is only the time if we all agree as such. Otherwise, now is not the time. For instance, right now it is nine thirty but it is only nine thirty because we've all agreed that it is nine thirty. Who was the first one to figure out time?

The earliest recorded Western philosophy of time was expounded by the ancient Egyptian thinker Ptahhotep, who said, "Do not lessen the time of following desire, for the wasting of time is an abomination to the spirit."

Ancient Greek philosophers, including Parmenides and Heraclitus, wrote essays on the nature of time.

St. Augustine, in his *Confessions*, ruminates on the nature of time, asking, "What, then, is time? If no one asks me, I know: if I wish to explain it to one that asketh, I know not."

Idealist thinkers, such as J. M. E. McTaggart in *The Unreality of Time*, have argued that time is an illusion.

The man has never read J. M. E. McTaggart, nor heard of him, but shares his views.

Albert Einstein said the only reason for time is so everything doesn't happen at once.

The woman says, Joyce fucking Kilmer.
The friend says, The tree fucker.
The man says, It's all the same, it's true. But we don't have time for this now. Soon we should have dinner. And no, I will not violate any trees or cars today.
The woman says, A dear happiness to women.
The man says, Who said that?
The woman says, Joyce fucking Kilmer.
The man says, Who's thirsty?
The friend says, I could use another.
The woman says, Of course you could.
The friend says, I want to see how many of these I can drink before I pass out.

The man says, No one can understand what liquor does to a body.
The woman says, I think I can understand it.
The man says, It affects everyone differently. Biology is beside the point.

Joyce Kilmer didn't say *a dear happiness to women*.

Perhaps he did say it out loud to someone, but it isn't his quote.

Beatrice said this to Benedick in *Much Ado About Nothing*.

The man and woman saw a production of *Much Ado About Nothing* during a Shakespeare in the Park festival.

The actress playing Beatrice was a full head taller than the actor playing Benedick.

Both the man and woman noted this but said nothing to each other about it.

Earlier that summer the same company put on *The Seagull*, by Anton Chekhov.

They didn't see *The Seagull*, though the woman suggested they try to get tickets. The man said he couldn't possibly get up early in the morning for such a thing.

The tickets to the Shakespeare were gifted by a friend of a friend of the woman, someone she protested with during last year's squabble with the board of elections.

When they saw *Much Ado About Nothing*, they brought a bottle of wine and packed a lunch and had a lovely time in the park.

Once swallowed, a drink enters the stomach and small intestine, where small blood vessels carry it to the bloodstream. Approximately twenty percent of alcohol is absorbed through the stomach and most of the remaining eighty percent is absorbed through the small intestine.

Alcohol is metabolized by the liver, where enzymes break it down. In general, the liver can process one ounce of liquor in one hour. If one consumes more than this, one's system becomes saturated, and the additional alcohol will accumulate in the blood and body tissues until it can be metabolized.

Though alcohol affects every organ of the body, it's most dramatic impact is upon the liver. The liver cells normally prefer fatty acids as fuel and package excess fatty acids as triglycerides, which they then route to other tissues of the body. However, when alcohol is present, the liver cells are forced to first metabolize the alcohol, letting the fatty acids accumulate, sometimes in huge amounts. Alcohol metabolism permanently changes liver cell structure, which impairs the liver's ability to metabolize fats.

For moderate drinkers, alcohol does not suppress food intake, and may actually increase appetite. Chronic alcohol consumption appears to have the opposite effect. Alcohol causes euphoria, which depresses appetite, so that heavy drinkers tend to eat poorly and become malnourished.

Alcohol is rich in energy, packing seven calories per gram. But like pure sugar or fat, the calories are void of nutrients. The more calories an individual consumes in alcohol, the less likely it is that they will eat enough food to obtain adequate nutrients.

This perhaps explains why these three haven't had dinner yet, though it has been ready for some time now.

Chronic alcohol abuse not only displaces calories from needed nutrients but also interferes with the body's metabolism of nutrients, leading to damage of the liver, digestive system, and nearly every bodily organ.

The woman says, He didn't answer my question.

The man says, What question was that?

The woman says, About the thrills, the seeking.

The man says, This man is always on the lookout, particularly when he looks out the window.

The friend says, I seek.

The woman says, What do you seek?

The friend reaches for the bottle of wine in the middle of the table.

The friend says, This'll do for now.

The friend pours another glass for himself, but doesn't offer to do so for the others.

The man says, He enjoys weather. He enjoys the bus. This we can safely say.

The friend says, Luckily, I never pass out on the bus.

The man says, You mean you haven't.

The friend says, That's what I said.

The man says, You said you never pass out on the bus.

The friend says, That's right.

The man says, What I'm saying is you haven't yet. Never is a long time.

The friend says, So you're saying I will pass out on the bus sometime.

The man says, That's not what I'm saying, no.

The friend looks at the woman. He pauses a moment as if he's trying to compose a question just so.

The friend says, Do you understand him when he talks?

The woman says, I'm afraid I can't say.

The friend says, Everyone is afraid around here. You're afraid you can't say. He's afraid he can't remember.

The man says, We all live in fear.

The friend says, There's no point arguing.

Some psychologists, such as John B. Watson, Robert Plutchik, and Paul Ekman, have suggested that there is only a small set of basic or innate emotions and that fear is one of them.

Fear is frequently related to the specific behaviors of escape and avoidance, whereas anxiety is the result of threats that are perceived to be uncontrollable or unavoidable. It is worth noting that fear almost always relates to future events, such as worsening of a situation, or continuation of a situation that is unacceptable. Fear can also be an instant reaction to something presently happening. All people have an instinctual response to potential danger, which is in fact important to the survival of all species. The reactions elicited from fear are seen through advantages in evolution. Fear can be a manipulating and controlling factor in an individual's life.

How fear first affects the body is through the brain structure that is the center of most neurobiological events associated with fear—the amygdala, located behind the pituitary gland. The role of the amygdala in fear is best understood as part of a circuitry of fear learning. It is essential for proper adaptation to stress and specific modulation of emotional learning and memory. In the presence of a threatening stimulus, the amygdala generates the secretion of hormones that influence fear and aggression. Once response to the stimulus in the form of fear or aggression commences, the amygdala may elicit the release of hormones into the body to put the person into a state of alertness, in which they are ready to move, run, fight. This defensive response is generally referred to in physiology as the fight-or-flight response, regulated by the hypothalamus.

Some of the hormones involved during the state of fight-or-flight include epinephrine and norepinephrine and cortisol. Epinephrine regulates heart rate and metabolism as well as dilating blood vessels and air passages. Norepinephrine increases heart rate, blood flow to skeletal muscles, and the release of glucose from energy stores. Cortisol increases blood sugar and helps with metabolism.

Everyone here is afraid, though it is unclear what exactly they all fear and why.

The fight-or-flight response has been either dulled or fueled by the alcohol.

The man says, You use the word *never* incorrectly. Never is never. Always.

The friend says, I don't understand.

The man says, This is what I was talking about earlier. We have to use our words. We have to make ourselves clear. That man in the park. The Irish singer.

The woman says, What is he talking about?

The friend says, His new lover.

The woman says, What?

The man says, He looked to be about fifty and wore an ill-fitted three-piece suit. He is one of those that's owned the same suit for years and only brings it out for funerals, showers, fancy Italian restaurants. He looked like an Andrew. Maybe his mother called him Andy, but she was the only one.

The friend says, She doesn't call him Andy anymore?

The man says, No, she died.

The friend says, That's sad.

The man says, She was sick.

The friend says, This is the Irish singer we are talking about?

The man says, I remarked on how much rain there had been and made a reference to Mount Ararat. He rearranged his face and grunted something unintelligible.

The friend says, I thought it was the Himalayas. Something about the Sherpas.

The woman says, What the hell are you talking about?

The man says, This was at the park.

The woman says, When?

The man says, Recently.

The chicken stew hasn't been stirred in an hour and is starting to coagulate.

It isn't ruined, though. Thus is the nature of stew.

The man will add some water to it later or tomorrow or whenever he remembers that he prepared a stew.

The friend says, The park is a good place to spend time if you are forced to leave the house.

The man says, There are usually people and dogs. I like to look at the dogs more than the people because you don't have to strain your neck.

The friend says, It's terrible.

The man says, The people at the park are usually boisterous or sullen, there's no in between. The dogs run and bark and slobber and misbehave like fucking dogs. It's typical misbehavior. There's comfort in it, reassurance perhaps. For every dog there is at least one people. One people tethered to the dog by a string. The other people sometimes people together in groups. They sit on blankets and eat picnic-style and listen to radios and laugh and play Frisbee, which are legitimate ways to distract one's attention from the inevitable.

The friend says, The inevitable is inevitable.

The man says, To the inevitable.

They touch glasses. The man doesn't drink. The friends removes the toothpick from his mouth and lays it on the table.

The woman says, What is inevitable?

The man says, Everything.

The friend says, It's troubling how inevitable it all is.

The woman says, This is too much.

The friend says, It's overwhelming.

The woman says, So, who was this Irish singer?

The man says, He said something about never having met the queen. I don't know which queen he was talking about. It probably doesn't matter. Maybe it was the Queen of Ireland.

The friend says, Is there a Queen of Ireland?

The woman says, No. She was beheaded last week.

The man says, It was in the papers.

The friend says, I never look at the papers anymore. This is what television is for.

A monarchical polity has existed in Ireland during three periods of its history, finally ending in 1801.

In 1800, the parliament of Ireland approved the political union of the monarchy of Ireland with the monarchy of Great Britain and incidentally voted itself out of existence. The united entity thereby created was known as the United Kingdom of Great Britain and Ireland. With this union, the independent existence of the crown of Ireland was ended. From 1801 until December 1922, Ireland remained in this political union. After that date, most of Ireland left to become the Irish Free State with the remaining part, Northern Ireland, electing to remain in the United Kingdom.

The friend isn't the only one who never looks at the papers anymore.

At least 120 newspapers have shut down in the last five years.

The man says, At any rate, I said to him, Start with a strict definition of never and work your way down. I said, Glance leftward, then rightward, then left again to make sure. This is the point where things break down. But not here, my friend, not here. I made sure to call him my friend. I remember Ben the mailman said anyone who calls you "my friend" isn't. He was like a father to me.

The woman says, Your father. I've been meaning to tell you.

Everyone looks at everyone else.

The woman says, I don't know how to say this.
The man says, Say what?

The woman looks at the man. There is a particular look on her face.

She is squinting ever so slightly.

This squint is hardly perceptible.

The man recognizes this squint, but no one else would.

It's as if she is thinking about what she wants to say, like she is organizing her thoughts, assembling the appropriate syntax and diction.

The man waits for her to say something.

It goes on like this for a while.

The man says, Use your words.
The woman says, He's in the hospital.
The man says, What?
The woman says, This morning.
The man says, What about this morning?
The woman says, He has cancer.
The man says, What?
The woman says, Your father has cancer.
The man says, I'm sorry?
The woman says, No, he was on the phone earlier. They said something about secondary progressive. Or they said it was aggressive. I can't quite remember.
The man says, When was this?
The woman says, He collapsed at home. He was doing one of his recitations and he collapsed. They rushed him to the hospital. He called from there. They're running tests, trying to figure out the best course of treatment.
The man says, You're kidding, right?

There is quiet. People are thinking. People don't know what to think.

The man says, You're saying this because…
The woman says, No.

People are looking at each other. It's as if they've never met, all three of them.

It's as if they've never been introduced or that they've known each other forever.

The man says, What you're saying is, my father has cancer?
The woman says, Yes.

The man says, You go from not knowing how to say this to saying my father has cancer and is in the hospital. That he collapsed.

The woman says, Yes.

The man says, I talked to him last month.

The woman says, Apparently he didn't want to worry you.

The man says, And this is how you tell me?

The woman says, I couldn't think of any other way.

The man says, When did he collapse?

The woman says, I'm not sure.

The man says, And when did he call?

The woman says, This morning. While you were napping.

The man says, Why didn't you tell me this earlier?

The woman says, I'm telling you now. I wasn't sure how to tell you.

The man says, You weren't sure how to tell me.

The woman says, Sometimes people are unsure of themselves. It's not a crime.

The man says, That's what you want to say now? That it's not a crime.

The woman says, They said it was stage three. Or four. He's an old man, he gets confused. I don't know.

The man says, You don't know?

The woman says, I'm afraid I don't. I'm sorry.

The man says, I don't believe you.

The woman says, Old men get confused. Old men get cancer. What's not to believe?

Cancer staging is the process of determining the extent to which a cancer has developed by spreading. Contemporary practice is to assign a number from I-IV to a cancer, with I being an isolated cancer and IV being a cancer which has spread to the limit of what the assessment measures. The stage generally takes into account the size of a tumor, whether it has invaded adjacent organs, how many regional lymph nodes it has spread to, and whether it has metastasized.

Stage III cancers are also locally advanced. Whether a cancer is designated as Stage II or Stage III can depend on the specific type of cancer; for example, in Hodgkin's Disease, Stage II indicates affected lymph nodes on only one side of the diaphragm, whereas Stage III indicates affected lymph nodes above and below the diaphragm. The specific criteria for Stages II and III therefore differ according to diagnosis.

Stage III can be treated by chemo, radiation, or surgery.

Stage IV cancers have often metastasized, or spread to other organs or throughout the body. Stage IV cancer can be treated by chemo, radiation, or surgery.

The friend is keeping his head down. He isn't drinking wine. He isn't sure what to do, where to look.

He wonders what his wife, Janice, might be doing at home. She is either prostrate or folding something up to put it away.

The man's father indeed has cancer. It started in his lungs but now has spread to his brain. This is why he collapsed this morning.

He has undergone both radiation and chemotherapy in the last six months.

He chose not to tell his son and daughter-in-law, as they've been somewhat estranged for years.

The woman had walked in on him at the cabin when he was in the middle of someone.

He then made a series of crude and suggestive remarks to his daughter-in-law.

The woman chose not to tell her husband what she saw and what her father-in-law suggested.

The husband had sensed something was wrong when she returned from the cabin that weekend, but he didn't want to know about it.

He figured what he didn't know couldn't hurt him which is a cliché he's always tried to observe.

For the sake of fair play, let's say this is how it all happened.

Next time perhaps it's the father walking in on the woman in the middle of someone. She isn't the type to step out on the man, but people change.

Things happen to people and they change as a result.

It's something akin to causality or evolution, but not quite as specific.

The woman says, How many of your uncles had cancer? Your cousins? Surely this is not a surprise. Surely, you've been expecting this.

The man doesn't answer these questions. He is looking at his wife, the woman he is married to.

The woman says, I don't know what to tell you.
The man says, You don't know what to tell me?
The woman says, Your father. The man who raised you. The man we haven't seen in a long time because he's slowed down, you say. The

man who owned the log cabin upstate, the man who was in and out. He called. He said he has cancer. He said it was bad.

The friend says, I think I should go. Janice is probably worried.

The woman says, No, you should stay here. There's going to be stew and your wife doesn't strike me as the worrying sort. No, I'm sure the darling is just fine. I'm sure she is home alone and dancing naked and having a fine old time. I'm sure she hasn't a care in the world. You mustn't worry because, after all of that worry, what good does it do?

The friend says, She hasn't been feeling well.

The woman says, She's a free spirit. That's all. It's normal. People let you know when they don't feel well. They complain. Certainly your wife would. She doesn't strike me as strong or silent.

The friend says, This is a bad time. I should go. I'm drunk.

The woman says, Yes, indeed. You are drunk. You are often drunk. But it doesn't matter. None of us can understand what liquor does to a body, though we are pretty sure it makes you drunk. Listen. I want you to stay. So does Charlie Stewman. We both want you to stay. This is not something we are afraid of. We might live in fear like everyone else in the world, but this we are not afraid of. We don't care that you're drunk. Have another, please. Make yourself at home. Don't you want him to stay, darling?

The man says, I don't believe it.

The woman says, Yes, of course you do. See? We both want you here. It's always better when someone's watching. A third party, someone impartial. Someone who can report the goings-on, someone who can testify. A witness. Be a witness. This is how it should be and you both know I'm right.

No one responds to this. No one takes a drink of wine.

The three sit around the table like this for hours, days, years.

The stew remains in the pot, unstirred.

The car is still parked on the street in front of the house and will remain there indefinitely.

The man's father will be dead in less than a month. Such is the nature of cancer, particularly when it has spread to the brain.

Outside, no one passes by, either on foot with dogs or in cars or buses.

There are birds flying around, though, a flock of starlings, flitting from tree to tree.

The author gratefully acknowledges Steve Gillis, Dan Wickett, Guy Intoci, Michelle Dotter, Michael Seidlinger, Peter Markus, David McLendon, and Wikipedia.